Fabulous Phoebe

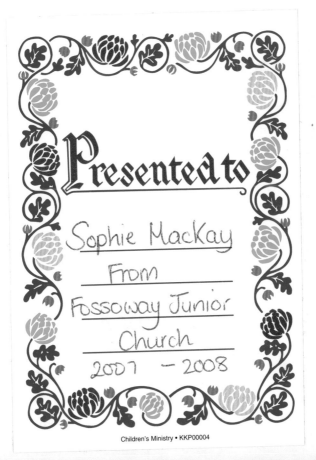

Presented to

Sophie Mackay

From

Fossoway Junior

Church

2007 — 2008

Children's Ministry • KKP00004

Other books in the Phoebe series:

Phoebe's Fortune
Phoebe finds her feet
Phoebe's Book of Body Image, Boys and Bible Bits

Also by the same author:

Deadly Emily
Flood Alert!
Seasiders: Runners
Seasiders: Liar
Seasiders: Joker
Seasiders: Winner
Seasiders: Angels

Copyright © Kathy Lee 2003
First published 2003, reprinted 2004
ISBN 1 85999 678 7

Scripture Union, 207–209 Queensway, Bletchley, Milton Keynes,
MK2 2EB, England.

Email: info@scriptureunion.org.uk
Website: www.scriptureunion.org.uk

Scripture Union Australia
Locked Bag 2, Central Coast Business Centre, NSW 2252
Website: www.su.org.au

Scripture Union USA
PO Box 987, Valley Forge, PA 19482
www.scriptureunion.org

British Library Cataloguing-in-Publication Data.

A catalogue record of this book is available from the British Library.

Printed and bound in Great Britain by Creative Print and Design (Wales) Ebbw Vale.

Cover design: PRE Consultants Ltd

 Scripture Union is an international Christian charity working with churches in
more than 130 countries, providing resources to bring the good news about Jesus
Christ to children, young people and families and to encourage them to develop
spiritually through the Bible and prayer.

As well as our network of volunteers, staff and associates who run holidays, church-
based events and school Christian groups, we produce a wide range of publications
and support those who use our resources through training programmes.

Contents

Chapter One

The size of the problem

"It's just puppy fat. Don't you worry."

Puppy fat! I hate that. It sounds like a disgusting delicacy eaten by Eskimos or starving Arctic explorers. Whale blubber... walrus meat... puppy fat.

They've been telling me about it ever since that awful day in junior school. It was the most horrible day of my life (up till then – I've had worse ones since, much worse).

In Maths, we all had to weigh and measure each other, and plot the results on a graph for the entire class. Miss West – who would never win a prize as Most Sensitive Teacher – pointed out that weight was usually linked to height, "apart from a few odd individuals". She pointed to my mark on the graph. It was high above the nice straight line she had drawn; it floated up there like a fat balloon, separate from all the others. I was much too heavy for my height, and I knew it, and so did everyone else. I wanted to crawl right under the table.

"Don't get upset about it," Mum had said when I told her. "It's puppy fat. It will disappear as you go into your teens."

But it hadn't. By the time I was 13 I was reasonably tall (five foot seven and still growing), and I weighed... never you mind what I weighed. Let's just say I was the fattest girl in my class, in fact in the whole of Year 9. I once inscribed my name, Phoebe, on a table in the art room, and when I came back the following week, some kind person had added the word 'Phat'.

Fat Phoebe. Was that how everyone thought of me? Not Fabulous Phoebe or Funny Phoebe (I do have a sense of humour – you have to if you're overweight. Just like very tall men have to look out for low doorways, fat people can sense approaching fat jokes.) Not Friendly Phoebe or Fanciable Phoebe or Fair-haired Phoebe or Photogenic Phoebe. Fat Phoebe.

"Oh, why didn't my parents choose a different name?" I moaned to Ellie, my best friend. "If they'd called me... I don't know... Minnie, I might have grown up skinny. Skinny Minnie."

"Lean Leah," she suggested.

"Slim Kim. Slender Glenda."

"It could have been worse," she said. "At least they didn't call you Georgie Porgy, or Ellie the Elephant."

This made me laugh because Ellie herself isn't the least bit elephantine. She's more like a giraffe, tall and skinny (taller than all the boys in our year), with large hooves and big square teeth. The teeth are being pulled in by a brace, but she hasn't yet managed to find a treatment for her size 9 feet. Her eyes are her best feature – big and brown, with long giraffe-like lashes.

As for me, in case you were wondering, my hair is probably my best feature. It's naturally blonde and quite long. I hate having to tie it back in Science lessons, because my face looks all plump and round without a curtain of hair at each side. You can hide behind long hair and I frequently do.

My worst feature you already know about. Everything else about me is... well, fairly normal, I suppose. Nothing startling – I mean, I'm not repulsively ugly and I'm not drop-dead gorgeous. I am not a genius or an idiot. At parents' evenings, teachers never have much to say about me; they hardly notice me, that's why.

Anyway, this is me:

Name:	Phoebe Alice Tate.
Age:	13.
Sex:	Look, how many boys do you know called Phoebe?
Address:	18 King's Avenue, Sandersfield (dull commuter town where nothing ever happens).
School:	Sandersfield High.
Religion:	Christian. Yes, I know people always say that, even if they don't believe in anything much. But I am actually a Christian, I go to church, all that stuff.
Father:	James Tate, deputy head teacher (not at my school, fortunately).
Mother:	Susan Tate, part-time secretary.
Siblings:	Georgie (age 11), full-time pain in the neck. Josh (age 1), quite cute, really, on a good day.
Interests:	Officially my interests are reading, writing, music and cookery. Oh, and I might as well put swimming though I haven't bothered with that for months. In reality my time is spent watching TV, phoning friends, using the computer, eating and dossing about.
Ambitions:	Don't know yet. Except that I don't want to rot in Sandersfield for the rest of my life.

My best school subject is English. Actually, that's one lesson where the teacher does notice me. Mrs Barclay always puts good comments on my work, and once she chose a poem of mine to enter in a national competition. It didn't win but it did get printed in a book. (Does that mean I can call myself a published author? Maybe I should have put this under Ambitions – to write a whole book of my own. Mrs Barclay says it's harder than you think.)

The lesson I really loathe is Games, which is dreadful from start to finish. Getting undressed in the big changing room where there's no place to hide... puffing and panting through the warm-up session... hopelessly failing to keep up with the class... collapsing in a heap, bright red and wheezing frantically... and no sympathy at all from the teacher, Miss Marne, who is a total sadist. More than once in her lessons I've thought – even hoped – that I was about to die. If I did, Marnie would get the sack and never be allowed to torture/teach again.

At the last parents' evening, Marnie made a comment about my weight. I was really annoyed. I mean, what's it got to do with her? It's not like she's a doctor or a dietitian.

She said to Mum, "You know, if Phoebe made a bit more effort, she might be quite good at hockey. She has an eye for the ball. I think she could make a good goalkeeper if she put her mind to it."

Yeah. I play in goal whenever I can – it means less running about.

Marnie turned to me. "But you know what's holding you back, Phoebe, don't you?"

I knew what she meant all right, but I wasn't going to admit it. "Those knee pads. They're too tight; I can hardly move in them."

Marnie scowled. "There's an answer to that. Lose some weight. You'd be a whole lot healthier and fitter if you could lose about three stone."

Mum said, for the hundredth time, "It's just puppy fat. She's only 13 and still growing, for heaven's sake. We don't want her to end up anorexic."

"Puppy fat?" Marnie, who is as thin as a barbed wire fence, looked at me and then at Mum. You could tell she was thinking that Mum, aged 38, hadn't managed to shed her puppy fat yet. But that was unfair; before she had Josh, Mum had always been... well, not slim exactly, but OK. She just hadn't managed to lose the extra weight from being pregnant.

"As for anorexia," said Marnie, "I'm not suggesting a crash diet or anything like that. Just cut back a bit and take more exercise. Exercise! That's the key!"

She must have noticed my lack of enthusiasm. "What about swimming?" she suggested. "You used to be quite good, I seem to remember. Weren't you on the school team in Year 7?"

"Yes, but I've gone off it," I muttered.

"Why?"

Because of people's nasty comments, that's why. "Look out, Phoebe's diving – she'll empty the pool! Phoebe, the great white whale... the bucket of lard..."

"I don't know. I just don't enjoy it any more," I said.

Marnie gave a deep sigh. "Well, find a sport you do enjoy. Or else walk more. Go for a twenty-minute walk every day – it won't kill you, I promise. Will you back me up on this, Mrs Tate?"

Mum nodded as if she didn't dare to argue. We went home, and I ate two orange Club biscuits to cheer myself up. That didn't work, so I had some crisps, a sandwich and a Coke, and felt slightly better.

Walking to the cupboard and back. Opening the fridge door. Lifting a glass... It's all good exercise, isn't it? Exercise. That's the key.

Chapter Two

A tight corner

Ellie has three stepbrothers. She acquired them when her parents split up and her dad remarried; his new wife was a widow with three little boys. Ellie named them the Three Monkeys because they were loud and cheeky and hyperactive. The worst thing was, they were always around when she went to spend a weekend with her dad.

"I could get on all right with Suzanne, if only she didn't have those kids," she complained. "She doesn't seem to realise how awful they are. Last week, Adam took my Walkman without even asking and broke the headphones, and then said it wasn't him. And she hardly even told him off!"

"What about your dad?" I asked. "Doesn't he ever say anything?"

"Not really. He wants them to like him, see. It would be different if he was their real dad."

"How old are they?"

She said, "They sort of go up in steps – four, six, eight."

"Well, obviously. They're your *step*brothers."

They lived on the other side of town, so I had never met them... that is, until the fateful day when Ellie rang me in a panic.

"Phoebe! Help! I've got to babysit the Three Monkeys tonight. Dad booked to go to the theatre for Suzanne's birthday, and now their usual babysitter's ill. Dad practically got down on his knees and begged me to do it. But it's going to be a disaster – I just know it is."

"Oh, come on, it can't be *that* bad," I said. "They're a lot smaller than you."

"Not added together, they aren't. I bet they won't do a thing I say. Phoebe, will you do me a big big favour? Would you come and help? I mean, you've got experience of little brothers."

I didn't think my experience with Josh (aged one and hardly mobile yet) would help much with the Terrible Trio. But hey, what are friends for? Anyway, I wanted to see if they were really as bad as she made out they were.

When we arrived, the house was quite peaceful, apart from gunshots and screams from some video the boys were watching. They were absolutely glued to it, sitting in a row like those Russian dolls that come in different sizes. They all had freckles, fair hair and grubby knees.

"Now behave, you horrible lot," said their mother, looking glamorous in a black velvet dress. "It's very kind of Ellie and Phoebe to look after you, so I don't want you to cause any trouble, OK?"

They paid absolutely no attention; their eyes were fixed on a police car exploding in slow motion. They didn't seem to notice when the adults went out. In fact, they never moved until the video ended. Then, in an instant, a huge fight broke out on the sofa, with yells, machine gun noises, and cushions shooting across the room.

"Knock knock," said Ellie.

"Who's there?"

"Armageddon."

"Yeah, yeah – Armageddon out of here. Don't you think we should try to calm them down a bit?"

Ellie shrugged. "They're always like this. But it is Oliver's bedtime. Come on, Ollie! If you get your pyjamas on really quick, I'll read you a story."

11

The smallest monkey looked at both of us, sizing us up. "I want *her* to read the story," he said, pointing at me. I felt absurdly flattered.

He was really quite well behaved – probably because I was a stranger. He whizzed into his Batman pyjamas like Clark Kent turning into Superman. As a reward I read him Thomas the Tank Engine *and* Bob the Builder, and he gave me a goodnight kiss! He obviously went for older women.

So far, so good. I went downstairs to find Ellie arguing with Luke and Adam.

"Your mum never said anything about baths," she said.

"But we *always* have a bath on Thursdays," said Adam, the eight-year-old.

Luke suggested, "We could both get in at once. That would save time."

"Oh, all right then," Ellie said weakly.

When the bath was ready, they refused to get undressed in front of us. "Go away! You're girls. We don't want *girls* staring at us in the bath!"

Fair enough. But when we went out we heard them lock the bathroom door behind us. "Oh, well," said Ellie, "they can both swim. They're not likely to actually drown themselves."

"Pity."

Now Oliver emerged from his room. "I want a bath too," he said, looking sulky.

"Not tonight. You can have one tomorrow." I led him back to bed, trying to ignore the yells and splashing sounds from the bathroom. It sounded like a massacre in a crowded swimming pool.

After a while, Ellie called them to come out of the bath.

"No! We've only just got in!"

"You can't make us. The door's locked, ha ha!"

Manic monkey laughter. "We're staying here until the water goes cold, and they can't stop us!" The splashing and shouting began again.

"Listen!" I roared. "If you're not out of that bath in TWO MINUTES, we'll ring your mum on her mobile. She'll have to come home and miss her birthday treat. Is that what you want?"

It worked. There was a subdued silence. Quite soon the door was unlocked, and they both came out in damp-looking pyjamas. While Ellie chased them off to bed, I cleaned up the bathroom floor, which rather resembled a pond, or an 'indoor water feature' like on TV. Now, that was an idea – a TV makeover programme starring the Three Monkeys. Watch them transform an ordinary home into something quite unrecognisable! See the stunned reaction of the owners!

Suddenly Oliver appeared beside me. "Why can't I have a bath? They had one and I didn't. It's not fair!"

"Get back in bed *right now*," I told him furiously. He took one look at my face and scuttled away.

At last all was quiet. Ellie and I sat down with a well-earned drink and a snack – but not for long. We heard feet on the stairs, and Adam rushed in.

"Ellie! Oliver's gone in the bathroom and locked the door!" he shouted.

"So what's wrong with that?"

"He's filling the bath up, but he's not allowed to have a bath by himself – he can't swim yet!"

We raced upstairs and pounded on the bathroom door. "Ollie! Open up!"

"No. I want to have a bath like the big boys." His voice was quite obstinate.

We could hear the roar of water cascading into the bath. It was a huge, old-fashioned bath, certainly deep enough to drown a small boy if his feet slipped while getting in. Oh help! What a birthday treat for Suzanne – coming home to find her house flooded and her child drowned!

We tried to reason with him. We used threats and bribes. We tried to break the door down, but unlike doors in the movies, it didn't shatter into pieces at the first kick.

And now there was no sound from Oliver. All we could hear was the thunder of water, as loud and fierce as Niagara Falls.

"Ring Mum," Luke urged us.

Adam said, "He nearly got drowned once in the paddling pool, when he was little."

They stared at us with frightened eyes.

Ellie tried Suzanne's mobile, but could only get the answering service. She left a message – not that it would be any use. We needed help right now, or else… or else it might be too late.

I had a sudden idea. "The window! Does it open?"

"Yes," said Ellie, "but we'd need a ladder."

"In the shed," said Adam.

We rushed outside, hardly noticing that the boys were in pyjamas and bare feet. Together we dragged the ladder out and propped it against the wall. Then Ellie and I looked at one another. Ellie, despite being almost six feet tall, hates heights. They don't bother me, but I'm not the right shape for wriggling through windows.

"I'll do it," said Adam, shaming us into action.

I began to climb the ladder. Luckily it was a good, strong one, almost new. But the window looked old. It looked as if it wouldn't open without a struggle.

Holding on with one hand to the top of the ladder, using the other hand on the window, I managed to raise the lower sash by a few inches. It was dark inside – I couldn't see a thing.

"Oliver. Ollie! Are you all right?"

There was no answer. Nothing else for it... I would have to climb in.

Hard as I tried, I couldn't make the window open any further. It would be a tight squeeze. And I could not see what lay on the other side of the window sill. Would I end up going head first into the toilet?

I put my head in, squeezed my shoulders through, and let my eyes get used to the darkness inside. Oh, thank God – I could see Oliver. He wasn't in the bath, he was lying on the mat, curled up with his thumb in his mouth. The little toerag was sound asleep.

But the bath! The bath was just about to overflow. Quick, quick...

I heaved myself further through the window. My feet left the ladder and flailed about in the air. Using my elbows, I shoved against the inside of the wall, and got myself in as far as the waist. My stomach scraped painfully against the brick window sill.

Now we hit a problem area – my hips. I wriggled and squeezed, I put my hands flat on the wall and pushed, I sucked my stomach in and pushed again. But it was no good. The window was just too small.

I tried to go into reverse. Trouble was, going backwards there was nothing to push against. My arms waved about helplessly inside the room – on the outside my legs did the same. And the window frame pressed down on my spine, holding me like a mousetrap.

Yes, exactly like a mouse in a trap – I was stuck.

Chapter Three

Leo

"Help! Help!" I yelled, wondering if anyone could hear me down below. I kicked my legs wildly. Couldn't they see I was in trouble?

"Phoebe, are you all right?" Ellie's voice sounded far away.

"No – I'm stuck! Get the fire brigade or something. Quick!"

And now water was starting to slide over the edge of the bath. It splashed onto the floor quite close to where Oliver was lying. Oh, come on, Ollie, wake up! Open the door, turn off the tap, *do* something!

By this time I was actually in pain. The window sill dug into my stomach; the window itself was heavy on my back. I felt like a magician's assistant being sawn in half. (One way of losing weight.)

"Help!" I shrieked. "Help me!"

"All right, all right," came a stranger's voice from behind me. "But stop kicking, will you? I can't help you if you knock me off the ladder."

Two hands gripped me firmly above the knees. Someone began to tug me backwards. I moved a few inches, then got stuck again.

"The window," I gasped. "Can you open it a bit more?"

Whoever my rescuer was, he was strong. The window creaked in protest as he forced it further open. Now I had room to wriggle backwards through the gap, and his hands guided my feet onto the top step of the ladder.

He said, "OK. Can you manage to climb down? I'll go first."

Shakily I went down the ladder. At the bottom, I turned round to see who my rescuer was. To my surprise he was not much older than me. I vaguely recognised him from school – Leo somebody. Yes, Leo Jones, from Year 10.

Ellie grabbed my arm. "What about Oliver?"

"He's fine – he's asleep on the floor. But the bath! It's overflowing – there's water everywhere!"

"What's going on?" asked Leo.

We all tried to explain at once. As soon as he understood, he was off up the ladder again. Quick and agile, he slid in through the window like a cat slipping through a fence. But then his head appeared again.

He called, "I've turned the water off. But there's no sign of the boy."

"What?"

"The kid – he's not here! The door's open and he's gone."

Oh, terrific! Oliver must have woken up and let himself out. But where had he gone?

He wasn't in his bed. He wasn't in the kitchen or the living room. We searched the entire house, beginning to panic all over again. Finally Luke tracked him down, huddled inside a wardrobe. He was soaking wet, shivering and scared. I felt so sorry for him, I forgot to be angry.

But Leo was tougher. While Ellie got Oliver dried and changed, Leo gave him a good telling-off. Didn't he realise how stupid he had been? He might have drowned himself... he might have flooded the entire house... he might have seriously injured his babysitter. What if she had fallen out of the window and killed herself?

"She couldn't fall, she was stuck," Adam objected. He and Luke went off into fits of giggles, their arms waving frantically like my legs must have done.

"Shut up," Leo snapped at them. "Nothing funny about it! You wouldn't be laughing if it happened to you. Now get to bed!" To my amazement, they obeyed him at once.

But I had suddenly seen myself the way they saw me – big fat hips wedged in the window, big fat legs kicking helplessly in the air. I felt my face burn with embarrassment. Tomorrow the story would be all around the school. Phoebe got stuck half way out of a window! Leo Jones had to pull her out – pop, like a cork from a bottle! What a killer...

"I'll just go and mop up the bathroom," I muttered, and fled from the room.

A huge lake had covered most of the tiled floor, but fortunately it hadn't spread out onto the landing. I mopped it up fiercely, wishing it was possible to mop up the entire evening, wipe it away, get rid of it for ever.

Maybe I could persuade Leo not to tell anyone. I knew I could count on Ellie not to blab – she was my mate, and anyway I knew some embarrassing things about *her*.

When I had mopped up every drop of water, I listened at the door. Not a sound outside; Leo must have gone by now. I crept out and went looking for Ellie. She was in the kitchen getting a drink from the fridge.

"Oh, Ellie," I moaned, "what am I going to do? He'll tell everybody, I bet he will. How can I get out of going to school tomorrow?"

"Don't you worry." Leo's voice made me jump about half a mile. There he was, leaning on the breakfast bar and grinning at me. "I won't tell if you won't."

"Oh!" By now my face must have looked as red as a fire extinguisher. Lucky I hadn't said anything nasty about him. Even luckier, I hadn't said anything nice about him – because he was quite good-looking, tall and lean, with dark eyes and a confident smile. He was a Grade B or perhaps an A. I could tell that Ellie agreed with this assessment by the daydreaming look on her face.

"Do you want some free advice?" he said. "Next time you get asked to babysit for this lot – say no. They're a nightmare."

"I know that," said Ellie gloomily. "They're my stepbrothers."

Now it was his turn to look embarrassed. "Are they? Sorry, I didn't realise..."

"It's OK," she said, "I totally agree with you. They're horrible. But how do you know them? Do you live around here?"

"Yeah, in Lime Avenue. Our garden backs onto this one." He told us how the three boys kept kicking their football over the fence and climbing over to get it, trampling over anything in their way. When his dad shouted at them, they shouted back and threw stones at his greenhouse.

"People round here felt sorry for them at first," he said, "you know, losing their dad like that."

"What happened to him?" I asked.

"Killed in a train crash when Oliver was just a baby," Ellie explained.

I said, "It must have been pretty hard for Suzanne, bringing that lot up on her own. Before she met your dad, I mean."

"Yeah, and marrying Dad hasn't changed anything. I told you, he's useless with them. He buys them sweets all the time instead of telling them off."

"What's useless about that?" I asked. "Sounds to me like an ideal father."

Leo laughed, and suddenly I noticed something weird was happening. Here I was, actually talking to a Grade A boy – having a normal conversation, having a laugh. I wasn't feeling shy and awkward. I was not thinking carefully before I spoke, desperate to make a good impression. (It was far too late to make a good impression on Leo. He had already seen all my bad points.)

We talked for a while about parents, their problems, how to handle them. Then Leo said he had to go. He collected the skateboard which he'd left outside, stepped onto it and slid smoothly down the drive. "Thanks for your help," I remembered to say as he vanished in the darkness.

"Wow!" said Ellie, closing the door. "He's really cool. Not only good-looking but nice as well! He's an A."

"Might even be an A-star," I said.

We have this system for grading boys, you see – like GCSEs.

  A – Absolutely Adorable.
  B – Better than most.
  C – Could be OK, if…
  D – Don't bother.
  E – Excruciating.
  F – Friend of Frankenstein.

The problem is, A-grade boys expect to go out with A-grade girls. (You know – gorgeous face, good figure, hair like a shampoo ad, skin without a single spot. Brain cells an optional extra.) Ellie and I are not, if we're honest, any higher than a C. Could be OK. Could be OK, if… if I was thinner; if Ellie didn't tower over the boy in question.

"Do you really fancy him, then?" I asked her.

"Too right I do. How about you?"

I shrugged. "Yes, but what's the point? He would never like me in a million years. Not after hauling my fat backside out of a window."

Ellie giggled, then stopped when she saw my face.

"I've decided something," I told her. "I'm going to lose some weight."

Chapter Four

A walk in the park

"So how's the diet going?" Ellie asked me.

It was one of her weekends for staying at home, rather than going to her dad's. We were getting ready for a Saturday afternoon shopping trip. While Ellie put her eye make-up on, I sat on the bed and stroked her cat, a handsome grey Persian with silky soft fur. Ellie had named him Casper because of his mysterious, ghost-like way of vanishing and silently reappearing.

The diet... yes. It had started off really well: no more biscuits, no little snacks, Diet Coke instead of normal, carrot sticks instead of crisps. During the first week I lost four whole pounds! But in the second week, while still being strict with myself, I only lost two pounds. And now I was starting to get bored with the whole thing. I was longing, really yearning, for an orange Club biscuit or two.

"Six pounds altogether! That's great," said Ellie. She looked at me sideways. I knew what she was thinking: where exactly had the weight come off? The scales said I was thinner, but I didn't look any different. It was slightly easier to do my trousers up, but that was all.

At this rate it would take years to make a visible difference. And already I was sick of low-fat yoghurt, low-sugar cereal, low-calorie soup, low-taste everything.

The cat pressed himself against my hand, so I stroked him again. Cats are so lucky – they don't seem to have weight problems, not if they're allowed to roam around out of doors. But then if I ate nothing but Kit-e-Kat and dead sparrows, possibly I wouldn't have a weight problem either.

At last Ellie was ready to go out. She was wearing her new shoes, which made her even taller and would probably cripple her after the first five minutes of wearing them. "Oh, stop nagging," she told me. "You sound just like Mum."

However (just like a mum) I was right. Before we'd even reached the end of Ellie's road she was walking with a limp. She sat down on a garden wall and took one shoe off. While she was trying to rearrange her toes, I glanced at the garden behind her. It had five bird tables in it, all well stocked with bird seed and bags of nuts; there were two bird baths full of water, and dozens – hundreds – of birds. I'd never seen so many birds in one small garden. All different sizes, shapes and colours, they were pecking and squawking everywhere. I also noticed a handwritten sign on the wall: 'This is a bird sanctuary. Cats and squirrels KEEP OUT!'

The house belonged to an old lady called Mrs Bruce. Most people called her the Bird Woman for obvious reasons.

I pointed to the sign on the wall. "Is she nuts? She seems to think that cats and squirrels can read."

"Well, yeah. Maybe she is a bit loopy. Mum says she was OK until her husband died, but now she lives there all by herself, and doesn't talk to anyone except the birds."

We were coming to the gateway of the park. "Let's go this way for a change," I suggested.

"Why?"

"Er... it's the scenic route."

"Oh sure. I know exactly what scenery you're

thinking of. Rolling hills, deep valleys, glorious views of local wildlife in its natural habitat... You want to go past the skateboard ramps. Right?"

I nodded sheepishly.

The skateboard ramps were crowded, but only with little kids. I could see immediately that Leo wasn't there.

Ellie said, "I don't think he comes down here much. He goes street skating on kerbs and railings and things."

"How do you know?"

"Adam told me. He's seen Leo out in the street – Adam talks about him like he's some kind of hero. Adam wants to get a skateboard of his own and be just like Leo. Hey, can we sit down for a bit? My feet are absolutely killing me."

We sat down on a bench with a good view of the ramps, in case Leo did make an appearance. I really hoped he would, although I knew it was pointless. If he saw me, what did I expect him to do – come and talk to me, right there in front of all his mates? Most likely he wouldn't be seen dead with Ellie or me.

I had seen him once or twice at school. The first time, when we passed in the corridor, he grinned at me but didn't speak; all the same I felt myself blushing. The second time, I saw him but he didn't see me (or didn't want to see me). He was coming out of the RE room at the end of lunch hour. And that was odd, because the only lunchtime activity in the RE room was the school Christian Union, which I'd been to a few times before I got bored with it.

I wondered why on earth a boy like Leo would go to the CU. Maybe they were having a special debate. 'Skateboarding – right or wrong? Find out what the Bible says on the subject' (not a lot actually).

Was it possible that he was a Christian? I knew he

didn't go to my church, but there were several other churches in town. And he'd certainly behaved in a Christian kind of way when he came to my rescue. He had also kept his promise not to talk about it at school. Oh, he was so nice...

Ellie and I decided to go to the next CU meeting. I had warned her it would be pretty boring. "Not if Leo's there," she said hopefully.

After resting her feet for a while, Ellie was ready to get up again. We walked slowly through the park (I tried not to look at the ice cream van by the pond). As we were passing some bushes, Ellie suddenly stopped.

"Oh, not again," I muttered. "Why don't you just take your shoes off and walk in your bare feet?"

"Shush. I heard a funny noise – in there."

She was right. I could hear a strange sort of coughing, choking sound from somewhere in the bushes.

"It's someone being sick," I said, "spewing up ten pints of lager." At night the park was a well-known meeting place for under age drinkers... but not usually in daylight, at three in the afternoon.

Reluctantly I followed Ellie towards the source of the noise. "Oh," she cried, "it's a cat. The poor thing!"

"It does look ill," I said.

I had seen a cat being sick before, but not like this – not lying on its side, too weak to get up. Its stomach heaved as it retched again, trying to be sick. Nothing came out. There was a smelly patch of vomit nearby... oh, yuk. I didn't want to get too close.

But Ellie, who loves cats, crept nearer. "I wonder who it belongs to. It's got a collar and a name tag – look."

The cat was now lying still with its eyes shut. Gently Ellie lifted the name tag and read out, "Tigger, 354216. Must be a phone number – I'm going to ring the owner."

She rang on her mobile. Five minutes later, an anxious-looking woman arrived with a cat basket. The cat had not moved much while we waited; it mewed faintly as the owner picked it up, then it lay still again.

"Tigger, you are naughty," the woman said. "You've been eating something you shouldn't have. Off to the vet with you..." She thanked us and hurried away.

"I hope the vet can help," said Ellie. "I hope it's not too late." To me it looked as if the cat was dying, but I didn't say so. Ellie would only get upset.

We went on into town. Ellie tried on some jeans, which would have looked great if they were three inches longer. I found a top I really liked, but the shop didn't have it in a bigger size (story of my life).

By now Ellie's toes were actually bleeding, so we went into McDonald's for a chance to sit down. I only meant to have a Diet Coke. But somehow the sight and smell of food hypnotised me and took away all my willpower. "Big Mac, fries and a chocolate milkshake," I heard myself saying.

"What about the diet?" whispered Ellie.

"Shut up."

On the whole, not a good day, Saturday. As I'd already messed it up, I decided I might as well have an ice cream for pud. I told myself I could start again tomorrow.

Chapter Five

Miranda

Our school dinners aren't wonderful if you're on a diet. Salad is provided – the trouble is, it's always the same every day. Limp lettuce, weary-looking cucumber, a teaspoon of coleslaw and some grated carrot, served with rubbery ham or leftover pie. After a week of the diet I got so sick of it that I decided to take a packed lunch for a change.

I'd forgotten that packed lunches had to be eaten in the small dining room, away from Ellie and my other friends. Looking round for someone I knew to sit with, I spotted Miranda Frost. Although she wasn't a friend exactly (she was in my year but a different form), we had been going to the same church for years. Miranda's mum used to be our Sunday school teacher when we were little. I remember she was pretty strict, especially with her own daughter.

I don't think I've changed much over the years – I mean, you would recognise me in our ancient holiday photos. (I'm always the one holding the ice cream.) But something weird has happened to Miranda as she's got older. Like a fairy tale heroine under a spell, she's changed from being quite plain to startlingly pretty. She has a perfect, heart-shaped face, with model-girl cheekbones and huge, dark, shining eyes. It's so unfair. Why her and not me?

Her friends at school are girls like Lauren and Jade and Olivia. BBB, I call them – Beautiful But Bitchy. However, there's one good thing about being fat...

BBB girls don't see you as a rival, so they don't bitch about you. They hardly even notice your existence.

Jade and Olivia carried on talking as I sat down next to Miranda, who moved her lunch box rather grudgingly to make room for mine. She was surprised to see my healthy-looking lunch, and we talked about diets for a while. Miranda is one of those people who knows the calorie content of everything, although she doesn't need to – she's as slim as a panther.

"You shouldn't be eating bananas if you're slimming," she told me. "A pear or an apple would be better. And what's this – tuna in mayonnaise? Phoebe! Mayonnaise is ultra-fattening!"

I hate apples. I'm not too keen on tuna either, not without mayo. To change the subject, I asked if she knew what time the Christian Union meeting started.

Miranda sort of flinched and glanced quickly at her friends, who weren't listening. She looked relieved. I suddenly realised she didn't want them to know she went to church.

"I think it starts at one-fifteen," she muttered. "But I haven't been for a while. Dad and Mum keep telling me I ought to make the effort… but it's always so boring."

"Yeah, I know. I thought I might give it a go today, though. How about you?"

"I might," she said cautiously. Her friends were getting ready to leave; Miranda stood up too. "Bye then."

"Bye. See you on Sunday."

Oops! I shouldn't have said that. Miranda gave me an angry look as she went off with her friends.

I could see that she was living a sort of double life – like a secret agent. She had two quite separate groups of friends, at school and at church, and she didn't want to mix them, because she herself was a different person at school and at church. At school she was one of the BBB girls. At church she was a good little Christian, like her parents wanted her to be. But who was she really?

I went to find Ellie and we headed for the CU meeting. If Leo wasn't there, this was going to be a total waste of time. Please, oh please, let Leo be there...

He was! But he didn't see us. When we went in, he was with a small group of Year 10 and 11s who seemed to be rehearsing a bit of drama. This was something new – when old Sooty was in charge of the CU, we never did anything except sit around and talk. But Sooty had just retired and Mr Price, the new Drama teacher, had taken over. He might liven things up a bit.

Just as the meeting started, I saw Miranda slip into the room. She sat at the back near the door – I suppose a secret agent has to be ready for a quick getaway. But then I forgot her because Leo was talking.

"Greetings, Earth creatures," he droned in a computer-like voice. "I come from the planet Zarg. I come seeking knowledge. I study the religions of Earth. They are many and strange. I talk with sun-worshippers in Corfu, and followers of the Great God ManU. I visit temples to McDonald in every city. Now I must study Christians. Excuse me please – what is a Christian?"

The Earth creatures gave him various answers.

"A Christian is somebody who goes to church."

"Christians... er... they believe in God. I mean, the Christian God, not any of that other lot."

"Christians are morons."

"A Christian, well – I think you're a Christian if you got christened as a baby."

"A kind person that helps people."

"One of them Americans on the telly that asks you to send them money."

Leo, the alien, looked confused. I thought he was very good, a natural actor; I couldn't take my eyes off him. "Stop staring," Ellie muttered, nudging me.

When the sketch ended and Leo departed to the planet Zarg (aka the RE cupboard), I did try to listen to the discussion that followed. But I knew the answers already.

Q What are Christians? (Tick the correct answer)

𝒜 People who believe Jesus Christ is the Son of God.

ℬ People who know they've done wrong and ask God to forgive them.

𝒞 People who give their life to Jesus.

𝒟 All the above. ✔

I knew it all – I'd been hearing it since the year dot. But it was new to Ellie; her family don't go to church. She looked quite interested.

The interesting bit, for me, came right at the end. As we were helping to rearrange the tables and chairs, I worked my way closer to Leo.

"I thought you were really good in that drama," I said to him.

"Which drama? The planet Zarg, or your burglary attempt?"

"Shhh! You haven't told anyone, have you?"

"Of course not," he grinned. "Your secret is safe with me. How's that little kid behaving himself? Has he got into any more trouble?"

I said, "Not really – you must have put the fear of death into him. And Adam, his big brother, thinks you're wonderful. Ellie says he wants to get a skateboard just like yours."

"Oh, hi, Leo!" a voice interrupted. Miranda was standing right next to us, giving Leo the full brilliance of her smile. "Haven't seen you for ages. Have you given up on the Drama Society?"

"Yeah. I haven't really got time these days."

She gazed up at him with those big, soulful eyes. "That's a shame. We're casting the next production and we could use a guy like you. At the moment it looks like Max Butcher will be the male lead, and who wants to kiss Max Butcher?"

I had to admire the way she did it. Without actually saying so, she had told him: I'd much rather kiss you. But I felt my heart sinking like a half-baked cake. If Miranda liked Leo, the rest of us might as well give up and go home.

Leo, however, didn't seem interested. "Sorry," he said, "too much else going on." Then he turned back to me. "Talking of skateboards, I've got an old deck I don't use any more. Adam could have it for a fiver if he wants. I mean, it's not great, but it would get him started."

"You'd better ask Ellie," I said. "She's over there."

As he walked away, I happened to glance at Miranda. Just for a second I caught a look of sheer fury on her face. She wasn't used to being ignored like that. And she didn't like it one little bit.

I smiled to myself. In fairy tales, the beautiful people always get everything they want and live happily ever after. In real life they have to face a few disappointments, just like the rest of us.

"What are you laughing at?" she hissed.

"Oh – nothing."

She glared at me. "You fancy him, don't you? Well, you needn't bother, Fat Phoebe. He'd never go out with a big fat cow like you!"

Her voice was jagged with hatred, and it shocked me. I felt as if she'd punched me in the stomach without any warning. I couldn't speak. I just stared as she turned on her heel and marched out.

That was it. That was how I became Miranda's enemy number one.

Chapter Six

Cat walk

When I weighed myself at the end of the week, I had lost nothing at all. Zilch. Zero. Nil pounds.

I couldn't believe it – all that effort for nothing! "The scales must be wrong," I complained, stepping off and on to them again with exactly the same result.

Mum tried to encourage me. "This does happen sometimes on a diet. It's all to do with the amount of fluid in your body at different times of the month. Don't give up, love, you're doing really well."

"But I don't *look* any different. I look just as fat as when I started. What's the point?"

I felt so depressed that I sneaked a packet of crisps out of the cupboard. They tasted absolutely delicious – the first crisps I'd eaten for three weeks – and I went back to get some more. But then I thought of Leo and stopped myself. *"He'd never go out with a big fat cow like you."*

Maybe I ought to do more exercise like old Marnie had suggested. Swimming? No... not until I got thinner. The gym? You had to be a member, and that was expensive. Running? Kick-boxing? Oh come on – get real.

It would have to be walking... only I would feel stupid walking round the block on my own. I rang Ellie to see if she felt like taking a little stroll. "But don't wear those shoes," I warned her.

It was a mild spring evening. Mr Whitely from two doors down was out weeding his front garden. I was amazed that he could find any weeds to pull up; his flower beds always looked as neat as a garden centre catalogue. (Not like ours, which had about a thousand dandelions per square metre. A wildlife garden, Dad called it.)

Another neighbour stopped to talk to him, and as I was passing, she stopped me too. "I don't suppose you've seen my cat? She's gone missing – I haven't seen her for three days. She's black with white socks, and she's a nosy little thing. I wonder if she's got trapped in someone's shed or garage."

Mr Whitely promised to check his garden shed, and so did I, though you can't actually shut the door of our shed. No self-respecting cat would be trapped in there for more than two seconds. I went round the corner into Ellie's road, which runs parallel to mine. Here I noticed that someone had stuck posters on every lamppost:

'Lost. Large grey tomcat, torn left ear, missing tail tip. Answers to the name of Lucky. If you find him, please ring 865124. REWARD OFFERED.'

"All these missing cats," I said to Ellie. "What about Casper? Maybe you'd better keep him indoors for a while."

"Oh, I can't. He'd hate it. What do you mean, missing cats?"

"Well, I know of at least two, both local, both recently gone missing. Don't you think it's a bit..."

"Another thing," Ellie interrupted. "Old Miss Winter across the road – her cat died last week. He got ill suddenly and kept being sick, and before she got him to the vet he was dead. It reminded me of that cat we saw in the park."

"Maybe there's something going round," I said. "An epidemic. A Great Plague, killing off all the cats in the area. Those missing cats got it and just crawled away to die somewhere."

"How awful," said Ellie. "You're right, we ought to keep Casper indoors."

If it's not too late, I thought… if he hasn't caught the disease already.

"Where is he at the moment?" I asked.

"I don't know. He comes and goes by the cat flap without telling me what he's up to. Oh – there he is!"

Casper was walking regally along a garden wall. In response to Ellie's frantic calls, he leapt into action – streaking along the wall, diving into some bushes and disappearing.

"That's the trouble with cats," I said. "They only obey you when they feel like it. Not like dogs."

"Oh, dogs," said Ellie scornfully, "they're pathetic. They haven't got a mind of their own. I wouldn't have a dog if you paid me – I'm definitely a cat person. You must be a dog person, Phoebe."

I thought about this. "Not really. I'm not a cat or a dog person. Let's see… I think I'm an iguana person."

"What rubbish. You wouldn't recognise an iguana if it bit you on the leg."

Maybe not. But I do hate when people try to label you or put you in a box. Dog person – obedient, loyal, law-abiding. Star sign Leo – lively, extrovert, fond of attention. Fat girl – greedy, unattractive, no self-control. Teenager – rebellious and scruffily dressed. Christian – well-behaved, kind, rather boring…

Those labels don't describe real people like me. I don't fit into any of the boxes. (Yeah, yeah, they don't make them in my size.) I am unique, so don't try to label me, OK? Especially not with the F-word. No, not that F-word, the other one. Fat.

We walked for half an hour or so. According to a slimming magazine that Mum bought me, this should have used up around 180 calories, or one-and-a-half orange Club biscuits. The thought was tempting, especially when I saw my sister Georgie stuffing her face.

How come Georgie isn't fat? She eats quite a bit and never does much exercise. Dad says she must have a different metabolic rate, burning up food faster than I do. And it's true she is a restless sort of person. Even as she lay on her bed watching *Top of the Pops*, her feet twitched and her fingers tapped.

Disadvantages of sharing a room with my sister:

1 She's twitchy.
2 She's incredibly nosy.
3 She borrows my things without asking. (She loves big, baggy T-shirts.)
4 I can't retaliate because her things don't fit me.
5 She's even more untidy than I am.
6 She stops me getting on with my homework.
7 She has 73 fluffy toys, which she can't bear to part with, mouldering away on a shelf above her bed.

Only one of the above (guess which one?) gets any sympathy from Mum and Dad. But there's not a lot they can do. We can't afford to move to somewhere bigger because houses are so expensive around here.

Georgie finished her Hula Hoops, tossed the bag inaccurately towards the bin, and said, "Guess who asked me out today."

"Count Dracula?" I said. "Dennis the Menace and Gnasher? The Thing from the Black Lagoon?"

"Ha ha. No... Tom Fisher."

"Wow. You don't mean *the* Tom Fisher — the axe murderer?"

"No, Tom Fisher in Year 8, stupid. But I said no because I'm still going out with Ben."

That's another thing — Georgie's had stacks of boyfriends. Not proper boyfriends (she's only in Year 7, for goodness sake). I mean, she talks about going out with them, but no one actually goes *out*. She just sees them at school and writes their names in felt-tip all over her pencil case.

All the same, it's annoying. I have never, ever had a boyfriend. Not unless you count a weirdo called Adrian Pugh, who was in Nursery with me and kept wanting to play kiss-chase. I wonder what happened to him? *He's* probably an axe murderer by now.

I'd give anything to have a boyfriend. Even a Georgie-type relationship would be better than nothing... but if I had a proper boyfriend, Miranda and her friends would really sit up and take notice. He would have to be at least Grade C, though. Grades D and E just make you a laughing stock. "What does she see in him?" "No, what does he see in her?"

But Leo would fit the bill all right. Leo would be absolutely perfect... I wish. I wish. I wish.

Chapter Seven

Eating out

After Ellie, my next best friend is Sarah McFee. I got to know her at church, not at school – she goes to St Margaret's, a private school for the daughters of the filthy rich. (Sarah says it's a bit of a dump actually. It costs thousands a year, but the meals are inedible and you have to have cold showers after Games.)

Sarah had a birthday coming up. Her parents were taking her to see the Royal Ballet – she's mad about ballet. She was also inviting some friends for a Chinese meal. I don't mean a takeaway, but a proper sit-down meal at the Happy Garden, which is quite posh. Like I said, they're rich.

Rather secretively, Sarah slipped me the invitation after youth group. "I wish I could invite everyone," she said, "but Dad says six is the limit. So I thought I'd have two people from school, two from ballet class and two from church. That's you and Miranda."

Miranda! A slight shiver went down my spine. I hadn't forgotten the last thing Miranda said to me, or the look in her eyes as she said it. But that was when she was in BBB mode. In front of Sarah she would probably be her other self – friendly, or at least polite.

I certainly hoped so, because behind my back Mum had got together with Miranda's mum and agreed to share lifts. At half past seven Miranda called for me, looking amazing in a slinky little black number. Anyone would think she was at least 16 (age, I mean, not size).

I longed to be able to wear something like that.

After trying on almost all the clothes I possessed, I'd settled for a black skirt and blue silk top, both ordered from what Georgie calls the Fat Catalogue. Mum said it looked very nice – which didn't reassure me one little bit. What would the others be wearing? If they were all dressed up like Miranda, I would look totally out of place.

In the car, Miranda was pretty quiet. But then neither of us got the chance to say much, because Miranda's mum could talk for England. She asked loads of questions and hardly gave me time to answer any. Was I enjoying school? Had I chosen my GCSE subjects yet? Did I still play the clarinet? Oh, what a pity. Didn't I think it was sad that Miranda had given up learning the flute? Such a waste of her talents...

She insisted on coming right into the restaurant with us, although the whole idea of the evening was a girls' night out – no parents. Miranda gave a kind of stifled sigh. "I wish she'd stop treating me like a six-year-old," she whispered.

"Have a lovely time, darlings, and don't forget – Phoebe's mum or dad will pick you up at ten. Bye!" At last she went away, thankfully without asking Miranda if she'd been to the toilet and had a clean hankie. When she was gone, Miranda seemed to relax a bit.

"Do you know why Mum came in?" she said to me. "So she could check that there wouldn't be any boys at this party. Or any alcohol."

"What about drugs?" I suggested. "Loud music? Satanic rituals?"

"Don't even *mention* the words. She's absolutely paranoid, my mother."

By now we were seated at a big round table. Miranda was on my left; beyond her were Sarah's dancer friends, Nicole and Serena. They were both slim and elegant, like long-legged flamingos. On my right were two girls from Sarah's school, and then Sarah herself.

Looking around, I was relieved to see that my clothes were OK. In fact if anyone looked out of place, it was Miranda. Her little black dress might be great (I'm guessing here) for cocktails at the Ritz; it was way over the top for a Chinese meal in Sandersfield. But she didn't seem at all embarrassed. She was her usual confident self, chatting to the ballet girls as if she'd known them all her life.

The menu arrived. Oh help! I hadn't a clue which choices would be good for my diet. It's easy with stuff you buy from Tesco – most of it has the calories printed on the wrapper. In a restaurant you just have to guess. Sweet and Sour Pork sounds fattening, but King Prawns with Vegetables might be OK. As for Kung Po Beef – who knows?

I suddenly realised that a silence had fallen. Everyone else had ordered; they were all waiting for me. "Chicken with Oyster Sauce," I said at random.

It didn't really matter, in any case. When the food arrived it was put on a sort of turntable in the centre, so that everyone could try a bit of everything. And all of it was delicious. I was starving; I'd only had slimming soup for lunch, which seemed like months ago.

"Now don't be a pig," I told myself sternly. But it was difficult, especially when people kept rotating the turntable thing, putting new temptations in front of me.

"You must try the duck, Phoebe," said Miranda. "It's gorgeous."

"Have some more rice," offered Serena.

I noticed that Nicole and Serena were eating very little. "We're dancers. We have to watch our weight," Nicole explained.

Miranda whispered something to them – I heard the word 'diet'. The two of them raised their elegant eyebrows, looking down their long thin noses at my far-from-empty plate. I ignored them and started chatting to the girl on my right. People said St Margaret's girls were snobs, but Chloe was actually quite nice. She liked the same books as me and the same sort of music.

As we talked, more food kept coming round. "Just one more spoonful," I told myself each time, "and then I'll stop." But it was all so nice...

Someone giggled. I turned round to see Miranda, Nicole and Serena, all trying to look innocent.

"What's so funny?" I demanded.

"Oh nothing," said Miranda.

Serena said, "Nicole and I had a little bet going. I bet her that every time there was food in front of you, you'd take some. So far I'm winning."

"Miranda tells us you're on a diet," said Nicole. "What diet exactly? Miracle weight gain diet – put on ten pounds in less than a week?"

"The sea food diet," I said. "I see food – I eat it." You have to try and laugh it off – show them they can't get you where it hurts. But I had suddenly lost my appetite.

Miranda said, "Have you actually lost anything yet on this wonderful diet?"

"Yes I have, as a matter of fact. I've lost six pounds."

"I hope you reported it to the police," Serena said. "You never know, someone might find your purse and hand it in."

"Six pounds – really?" said Miranda sceptically. "Keep it up, Phoebe. Soon you'll have a figure like a ballet dancer."

"A belly dancer, don't you mean?" said Serena, and they rocked with laughter.

Chloe gave them a disgusted look. "Just ignore them," she whispered. But it wasn't easy, especially when I kept hearing the odd phrase such as 'sumo wrestler' or 'tree trunk legs'.

When Sarah realised what was going on, she put an end to it by talking to Nicole and Serena about the ballet. This left Miranda with no one to talk to, which served her right. She had ruined what could have been a really nice evening. But why? That was what I couldn't understand.

Perhaps she was trying to impress Nicole and Serena. She thought they would like her if she gave them something to laugh about. And the something was me.

I was really glad when Dad arrived to take us home. The evening had been a bit of a strain – on my nerves and also on the waistband of my skirt. When I stood up, I felt the button suddenly pop.

No way was I going to let Miranda see what had happened. I left the button wherever it had fallen, and walked out with hands pressed firmly to my sides. (This was to stop the skirt sliding down to my ankles.)

Miranda hardly said a word throughout the journey, except "Thank you" as she got out. Even Dad noticed the atmosphere. "What's the matter?" he asked me. "Have you and Miranda fallen out?"

"You could say that. She's pretty weird these days. She changes from being quite OK to really horrible, just like that."

"Like Jekyll and Hyde in the film," said Dad. "You know – good Dr Jekyll keeps changing into evil Mr Hyde?"

"Yes. Exactly," I said.

"Sounds to me as if she's got a problem."

I thought to myself that I was the one with the problem.

Q What is the best way to react when Miranda sticks the knife in?

A Burst into tears and threaten to tell Mummy.
B Turn the other cheek, like in the Bible.
C Try to get a laugh out of the situation.
D Somehow find a way of hitting back.

Chapter Eight

A Lesson

Next day Ellie rang me up from her dad's house, inviting me over. I said yes at once. It was a long walk, but that might help to use up some of the hundred thousand calories I'd consumed the night before.

Also I wanted to tell Ellie what had happened.

Also I was bored, and also...

OK, I admit it. Also Leo lived at that end of town.

I knew he lived in Lime Avenue, so I went that way, although it was a bit of a detour. No sign of him. But as I turned the corner into Beech Lane, I heard that unmistakable sound – the rattle of a skateboard. Two skateboards, in fact. Leo was on one, with Adam, looking a bit unsteady, on the other.

Ellie, Luke and Oliver sat on the garden wall, an admiring audience. Whenever Leo did a trick, such as flipping his board and landing on it again, the little boys clapped and cheered. Whenever Adam fell off they laughed.

"Look, Phoebe!" Adam raced his board towards me, eager to show off. "Leo's been teaching me. I can nearly do an ollie – look!" He fell off again onto the road.

He didn't make any fuss, though. You had to admire the way he got up, gritted his teeth and got straight back onto the board. "Has he fallen off much?" I asked Ellie.

"Oh no. Not more than about eighty times."

"You don't call it falling off. You say *bailing*," Luke instructed me. "See what Leo just did? That's a kick-flip. And that's a 180."

"Incredible. A whole new language," I said. "Wonder if you can do it as a GCSE? It has to be easier than German."

"A skateboarding GCSE – great idea." Leo jumped up the kerb and slid to a stop beside us. Adam tried to copy him and fell off (sorry, bailed) for the eighty-first time.

"Did *you* fall much when you started learning?" I asked Leo.

"Yeah. Loads of times. I broke my wrist once, and messed up the ligaments in my knee."

"This must be why girls don't skateboard much," said Ellie.

Adam said, "Because girls are cowards and cry-babies?"

"Because girls have got more sense," I said. "I mean, even the world's greatest kick-flip only lasts a second. A broken wrist lasts for months."

I was pleased with myself for remembering the word 'kick-flip'. Had Leo noticed? I must get the Three Monkeys to teach me more of the language.

"But you can get injured doing any sport," Leo argued. "And skateboarding is worth it. The first time I ever did that five-set by the Town Hall, it felt amazing. There's nothing like it."

"Worth breaking bones for?" I said.

He nodded. "But I don't suppose you can understand unless you've tried it yourself."

The Three Monkeys hooted with laughter at this – the thought of me on a skateboard. Luke yelled, "Don't let her. She'll break the board in half."

"She would need a deck made of concrete," said Adam, "with wheels like an articulated lorry."

Suddenly Leo looked very angry. He scowled down

at the three of them. "Stop that. You little idiots! Shut up and stop laughing."

Adam said sullenly, "It was only a bit of a joke."

"A bit of a joke! You know what a bit of a joke can do to people? It can kill them."

All of us stared at him. I thought he was overdoing it a bit. But then I didn't know what he was about to say.

"I used to have a cousin called Hannah. She had something wrong with her eye and she was waiting for an operation to put it right. It made her look cross-eyed, so people at school used to laugh at her. Just because she looked a bit different from everyone else, they called her names. Said she was ugly and she'd never have a boyfriend. 'We were just having a bit of a laugh,' they said afterwards. 'We didn't think she minded.'"

He took a deep breath. "But she did mind. One day she swallowed a whole bottle of sleeping pills... and she died."

There was a silence.

"That's awful," said Ellie.

Leo said, "Never laugh at people because of how they look. You can really hurt them. Understand?"

The three boys nodded dumbly.

"I've got to go now. See you." And he was off down the road.

"That was *your* fault," Adam said angrily, pushing Luke.

"No it wasn't. You said things too." Luke pushed him back. Adam tripped over his skateboard and went flying yet again.

"Oh, leave them to it," said Ellie, and we went indoors.

I couldn't make up my mind how I felt about that little episode. There were good and bad sides to what Leo had said.

Good:	Unlike a lot of boys, he was sensitive and caring.
Bad:	Any girl in his life would come second to his skateboard.
Good:	He understood that looks weren't everything.
Bad:	He thought I was like his cross-eyed cousin – odd-looking, a freak.
Good:	He stopped the boys from laughing at me. (Maybe he liked me?)
Bad:	He would have done exactly the same if I was bald, horribly spotty, had huge ears and/or goofy teeth.

Oh, and one more Good: He'd made a great impression on the Three Monkeys. They were very polite to me for the rest of the day.

Later on I walked home, feeling proud of myself. Ellie's dad had offered me a lift, but I'd refused it. Wow – I would soon be so fit I could run a Marathon.

I had left rather later than I should have, though. By the time I reached the town centre, dusk was falling; it was quite dark before I got home. I hurried through the empty streets, past gardens filled with darkness, shadowy hedges and crouching shrubs. If this was a movie, I would have been accompanied by ultra-scary music. But all I could hear was trees rustling in the chill night breeze.

All at once a ghastly screeching noise arose from one of the gardens. I leapt about half a mile into the air. Someone was being murdered! What should I do? Run? Shout for help? Call 999?

I scrabbled to find my mobile in my bag. Then a dark

shape shot over a wall and streaked across the road. It was a cat. That dreadful cry had been the screech of a cat, not a human. Thank goodness I hadn't rung the police – I would have looked a complete idiot.

All of a sudden a voice came out of the darkness. "That'll teach you," it said with a cackling laugh. "That'll teach you a lesson. Stay out of my garden!"

It sounded strange, the voice. It sounded slightly crazy. And who was it talking to – the cat?

Suddenly I realised where I was. Just ahead was the Bird Woman's house; I could see the notice on the wall telling cats to keep out. I crept forward in the shadows, until I could peep round the corner of a hedge. The front door of the house stood open. A light was on inside, with a dark figure silhouetted in the doorway – a little, hunchbacked old woman.

But what was that in her hand? Surely not... a gun?

I only glimpsed it for a second. Then, with another bone-chilling cackle of laughter, she hobbled inside and shut the door.

This must be the reason why cats were going missing. The Bird Woman shot them when they trespassed on her garden! No... surely not. How would an old lady get hold of a gun? And I hadn't actually heard a bullet being fired. Perhaps it was only an air pistol. I wondered what an air pistol could do if it was fired at close range.

Anxiously I went looking for the cat, but it had vanished in the night. I just hoped it would manage to find its way home.

Chapter Nine

Problem page

"A *gun*?"

Mum and Dad looked at me, gobsmacked. "Are you sure, Phoebe?" asked Dad.

"I can't imagine old Mrs Bruce with a gun," Mum said firmly. "She may be a bit – well, a bit eccentric. But she's not a raving lunatic."

Dad said, "Tell me what it looked like. Are you talking about a handgun or something bigger, like a shotgun?"

"A sub-machine gun?" said Georgie, grinning. "A nuclear missile?"

"Shut up, Georgie. It looked like a handgun. But I only saw it for a second."

"Bang bang!" shouted Josh. He understands a lot of words, though he can't say many yet apart from 'Mum-mum', 'Dad-dad', 'Beebee' (me) and 'Brrm-brrm' (anything on wheels).

"The cat – was it hurt?" Mum asked.

"I don't know. It did sound as if it was in pain. But then it shot across the road like a... like a bullet. Would it still be able to do that if it had been shot?"

"Depends where it had been hit, and what with," said Dad. "She might have used something like a BB gun. I've had to confiscate a couple of those at school. They fire pellets that can sting a bit, but unless you get one right in the eye, they don't actually do much damage."

"That sounds more likely." Mum sounded relieved.

"It's still cruel, though," I said angrily. "We ought to

report her for cruelty to cats."

Georgie, always up for an argument, joined in. "I don't think she did anything wrong. She was only protecting the birds. Look what cats do to birds when they catch them – torture them slowly and kill them bit by bit. *That's* cruel."

We argued about it for ages. Dad said it would be pointless going to the police, since pellet guns weren't illegal.

"We should report her to the RSPCA," I repeated.

Mum looked uneasy; she hates causing trouble. "I think you should leave it. You don't even know that Mrs Bruce hurt the cat – you didn't actually see anything, did you? Perhaps she just shooed it away, out of her garden."

I had to admit that this was possible. The gun might have been a toy that she waved around as a threat. She seemed to believe that cats could read, so she probably thought they knew what guns were. And of course I might have been mistaken about the gun. I hadn't really seen it properly.

When I told Ellie about it, she said, "So you're not going to do anything? You're just going to let her get away with it?"

"I don't see what I *can* do."

"We can keep an eye on her. See if she does it again."

So the next evening we walked past the Bird House, pretended to put a letter in the nearby postbox, and stood there for a while, talking innocently. What we needed was a cat invading the garden, but there were no cats to be seen. I suggested we could pop Casper over the wall.

"What? And let him get shot at?" Ellie was outraged.

"Only joking."

It started to rain. "Cats don't go out in the rain much," said Ellie. "They don't like it."

"How sensible of them."

We went home.

The next Christian Union meeting was unusual. It was called 'Problem Page'. Anyone who wanted to could write down a problem, without giving names, for the group to discuss.

"This boy I know, he's really great," I wanted to write. "How can I make him like me?" But of course I couldn't write this – Leo was in the room, and I knew I would blush bright scarlet if my question was read out. In the end I left my sheet blank. (Leo was writing something, though; I wished I could look over his shoulder.)

The papers were folded up, and two or three were selected at random.

'My friend often nicks things from shops. She dared me to steal a CD, and I did, but now I wish I hadn't. What should I do?'

We talked about it, each of us wondering who had written it. Same with the next one:

'My stepfather is a pig. I really hate him – we argue all the time. I wish my mum had never met him.'

For this one, people came out with all the usual Christian ideas. It's wrong to hate... perhaps if you treat him right, he'll treat you right... And Mr Price read out that verse from Matthew's Gospel: "Do for others what you want them to do for you."

I was amazed to see Miranda nodding agreement at this. Do for others what you want them to do for you! So you want people to laugh at you, Miranda, is that right? And make you feel like a fat, ugly sumo wrestler with legs like tree trunks?

Rage began to mount inside me, hot and stinging like heartburn. She was so two-faced! How could she behave like that and call herself a Christian? If only people knew what she was really like, they'd chuck her out of the CU!

"Time for just one more question," Mr Price said, unfolding it.

"'Someone I don't like much is in love with me, and keeps following me around. How can I get rid of this person without being rude to them?'"

Now who could have written that? Although the person had carefully avoided writing 'he' or 'she', I'd have bet a tenner that a girl wrote it. Your average boy wouldn't care about hurting a girl he didn't like. He would tell her to get lost, and laugh about it.

But Leo wasn't an average boy. A horrible thought hit me like a car door slamming on my hand. Had Leo written that? In love... following him around... was he describing me?

But when I dared to glance at him, I decided he had nothing to do with the question. His face showed mild boredom, very hard to act convincingly. He was probably miles away, landing a perfect 360. Miranda, on the other hand, was sitting quite still, as tense as a cat stalking a bird, her eyes fixed on the floor.

Now I felt sure that Miranda had written the question – and I could guess who she was talking about. His name was Simon Murphy, usually known as Smurf. He was a big, lumbering boy who everyone thought had the face of a troll and the brains of a squashed woodlouse. Everyone in Year 9 knew that Smurf liked Miranda; everyone (except Smurf himself) knew he was wasting his time. It's only in Disney films that a beauty and a beast become an item.

Lots of advice was offered: tell the person straight out – it's less cruel in the long run; ignore them and they'll go away; write a letter explaining how you feel.

Miranda said, "But what if… er, whoever it is… has already tried all those things and none of them worked? The boy still keeps following her around – you could almost say stalking her. In fact she sometimes feels quite scared of him. What should she do?"

The discussion continued, but I'd stopped listening, for I'd had an idea – quite stunning in its brilliance and simplicity. If I really wanted to get back at Miranda, it would be easy. Talk to Smurf (he was in my form, so I saw him every day), and tell him Miranda really loved him, but she had to hide the fact because her parents were so strict. He was dumb enough to believe anything. He would follow her even more closely, love her more desperately… embarrass her, frighten her…

No. No, I mustn't do it. I would be just as bad as Miranda if I behaved like that. But it was a tempting thought… more enticing even than an orange Club biscuit.

Miranda was speaking again. "It's like he's obsessed. He follows… er, the girl… home from school and hangs around outside her house, even when her parents threaten to call the police."

By now it must have been obvious to everyone, even the teacher, that Miranda was the girl in question. Leo, I saw, had lost his bored expression and was gazing at her with concern. She was making herself out to be like a film heroine – in danger, needing protection, threatened by a crazed knife-wielding stalker.

But this was ludicrous. It was Smurf she was talking about! If Smurf tried to threaten someone with a knife, he'd probably stab himself in the foot. He was far too slow and stupid and clumsy to be a good villain. If Leo knew the truth, he wouldn't waste his sympathy on Miranda, who didn't deserve it one little bit.

Suddenly the bell rang for the end of lunch, taking everyone by surprise. We hurried to sort out the chairs and tables. In the confusion, I got close to Leo.

"Hey, Leo," I said in a low voice. "Guess who it is that's obsessed with Miranda."

He looked blank. He was in Year 10; clearly he wasn't well up on the Year 9 gossip.

"It's Simon Murphy – Smurf," I said. "You know who I mean? The village idiot of Year 9?"

I could see he recognised the name. "The guy who smashed his bike into the Head's car? The guy who set fire to himself in the Physics lab?"

I nodded. "Personally, I think Miranda's overreacting. I mean, Smurf is a dangerous person – to himself, not to anyone else... But then Miranda's the dramatic type. She likes a bit of excitement in her life."

I turned away, feeling I'd said enough.

I was right. I'd said more than enough. Miranda was standing right behind me – and judging by the look on her face, she'd heard every word.

Chapter Ten

Hitting and stopping

After that things went rapidly downhill. Whenever she saw me Miranda was openly hostile, and so were her school friends. I couldn't even walk past them in the corridor without hearing snide remarks.

"If fear of spiders is arachnophobia, what's fear of fat people?"

"Phoebephobia."

Once I would have laughed at that – not now. I was losing my sense of humour. But that's all I was losing. I didn't manage to shed any weight at all for two weeks running; then, in the third week, I gained a pound. This was because I was so depressed that I'd been eating biscuits to comfort myself. (It worked, but only for five minutes at a time, so I had to keep going back to the biscuit tin.)

"Oh, Phoebe," Mum sighed. "And you were doing so well! What's gone wrong?"

"I don't know," I muttered.

She looked at me more closely. "Are you OK? Is everything all right at school?"

"Yeah, yeah."

It would have been pointless telling her about Miranda. Like I said, Mum hates making trouble. Especially with people that she knows. Even more so with people from church.

"Don't worry, Mum," I said. "I'm OK, really."

I went in search of an orange Club biscuit, but Mum had stopped buying them. I had to have two chocolate digestives instead.

Who cared if I was overweight? Leo would never love me, even if I was as thin as a racing bike, unless I was shaped like a skateboard and had four wheels attached to me. As for Miranda, she would still hate me and find hurtful things to say whether or not I lost weight. So why should I bother even trying?

Positive aspects of being fat:

1 You can eat whatever you like.
2 You don't have to wear a padded bra.
3 Everyone assumes you are friendly and jolly, with very little effort on your part. (I mean, what has Father Christmas ever said apart from "Ho ho ho"?)
4 You don't feel the cold. Fat is a wonderful insulator – ask any whale.
5 You don't waste your money trying to keep up with the latest fashions (not available in size 20).
6 You will never be broken-hearted when some boy dumps you.
7 On a desert island, you would survive longer than all the skinny people. (Unless they decided to kill you and eat you.)

But the next Games lesson forced me to have a rethink.

The whole of Year 9 did Games together, choosing which sport to do. Ellie picked netball; I had chosen hockey, and so had Miranda. To avoid her catty remarks in the changing room, I got changed in the toilets and lurked in there for as long as I dared.

When I finally made it on to the pitch, the lesson had already started. People were in pairs, practising hitting and stopping the ball – all except Miranda, who didn't have a partner. My heart sank into my mud-stained boots.

"Come *on*, Phoebe!" yelled Miss Marne. "Get a move

on, you've wasted half the lesson. Hitting and stopping! Give it some oomph!"

Miranda gave it some oomph all right. She hit the ball hard, at a wide angle, so that it shot past me way beyond my reach. It ran down a steep, muddy bank onto the lower pitch, where the Year 9 boys were playing football. I had to fetch it, slipping and sliding on the downward trip, puffing and panting as I came back up.

Next time Miranda hit the ball, the same thing happened. "Oops! Sorry!" she said, and then did it again. And again. Surely even the teacher could see she was doing it on purpose? But Marnie was at the far end of the field, not taking a blind bit of notice.

After my fourth climb up the bank I could feel my heart pounding away like a prisoner hammering on a cell door. My face, I knew, was bright red and shiny with sweat; my legs were black with mud. The footballers nudged each other and grinned as I invaded their pitch yet again.

"OK, that's it," I said to Miranda. "We're changing places."

She obeyed me; she must have seen how furious I was. Before she got in position, I gave the ball a mighty whack onto the lower pitch. Unluckily, Marnie saw me do it.

"Phoebe! What do you think you're playing at? Your partner hadn't a chance of stopping that ball. No, Miranda – let Phoebe fetch it. The exercise will do her good."

Wheezing like an elderly asthmatic, I staggered up the bank yet again. I must lose weight, I really must. This was killing me...

At the top, the first thing I saw was Miranda's triumphant smile. And the second thing – oh no – Leo. He was with two other Year 10 boys, inspecting the weather station at the side of the hockey pitch. He gave me a startled glance, then looked away.

Maybe he hadn't recognised me. Maybe he didn't connect this scarlet, gasping, mud-blackened figure with the Phoebe he knew... I would simply ignore him and hope he ignored me.

"OK, Phoebe!" Miranda shouted at the top of her voice. "I'm ready!"

Leo looked again. He did recognise me, I was certain. But he didn't speak or smile. Perhaps he was afraid of embarrassing me – more likely, he didn't want the other boys to realise that he knew me.

Oh, I could have killed Miranda! Taking careful aim, I whacked the ball as hard as I could, straight at her.

"That's *much* better, Phoebe," old Marnie said approvingly.

A different diet – that might help. A friend of Mum's recommended Quick-Slim milk shakes. Another friend swore by the Cauliflower Soup Diet, "except that it gives you the most dreadful wind".

I flicked through loads of diet books and magazines, all giving different advice. Cut out carbohydrates. No, eat carbohydrates but cut out fats. No, forget that, just eat tons of fibre to fill yourself up. Don't eat proteins and carbohydrates together. Don't do this, don't do that. Oh, and drink gallons of water (that was about the only thing they all agreed on).

Mum had started going to a slimming club that met every week. I went with her once, to see what it was like. But I was the only person there below the age of 30, and I felt as if everyone was staring at me. "I'm not going back there," I said.

Mum said, "Even if you don't go to the club, you could still follow the diet plan. We could do it together."

"Yeah, maybe," I said without enthusiasm.

"Oh, Phoebe." She put her arm around me. "It's really getting you down, this, isn't it?"

I nodded. I could guess what her next words would be: Let's pray about it. That was her answer to everything when I was little. And when I was little, I really thought it worked.

But as I got older I began to see that God didn't always give us what we prayed for. Even when we got a result, it usually came from other people or our own efforts – not from God. Was there actually any point in praying?

"Dear Father," Mum said, "you know how Phoebe feels about this and how much she wants to lose weight. Please help her to do it. Amen."

I could picture Mum's faith in God as a warm, glowing fire, with prayers going up like bright flames. My own faith was more like a flickering candle, almost blown out by the wind. My prayers wavered like a thin trickle of smoke.

Did God really exist? I had been brought up to believe in him because my parents did. What if they'd got it wrong, though? Perhaps there was no God, no loving father – no one to hear our prayers.

"Oh, God," I prayed silently, "are you really there? Can you hear me? Please, please help me to lose weight. If you do, I'll believe in you totally. I will – I promise."

Chapter Eleven

Blind alley

"MYSTERY POISONER," the headlines blazed.
"THREE SUSPICIOUS DEATHS."

Shock! Horror! That kind of thing just doesn't happen in Sandersfield, so the local paper made the most of it, with headlines right across the front page. It was only when you read the small print that you realised the victims were not humans, but cats.

A local vet had treated several cats that suddenly got very ill. Three of them were so sick that they died; another two slowly recovered. All the cats came from the same part of Sandersfield, the south west – where Ellie and I lived.

After the third death the vet was really worried, so he sent samples away to be analysed. The cat's body contained a poisonous chemical called organophosphate, often found in fly-spray and fertilisers. It was too late to find out if the other cats had eaten the same thing; their bodies had already been cremated. But they had shown the same symptoms – dribbling at the mouth, staggering, being sick.

"Listen to this," I said to Ellie. (It was the start of the Easter holidays and I'd gone round to her place, taking the newspaper to show her.)

"Vet Michael Welch believes someone is deliberately poisoning the cats of Sandersfield. He advises all cat owners to be extra vigilant. 'Use a recognised make of cat food, or meat that you have cooked. And it would be safer to keep cats indoors until the source of the poison is found. When they're roaming around outside, you have no idea what they may be eating. A tempting bowl of cat food could contain deadly poison.'"

"That's really sick," said Ellie fiercely. "Poisoning cats on purpose! Whoever did it should be made to eat the stuff themselves."

"If they ever get caught," I said.

Ellie looked worried. "Yes, what if they don't get caught? I can keep Casper in for a few days, but he won't like it. I can't lock him up for the rest of his life."

"Then we need to find out who's doing it," I said. "And I've got an idea. Who do we know around here who doesn't like cats?"

"The Bird Woman," Ellie said at once. "But hold on. If she started putting out plates of poisoned cat food, people would notice. Everyone knows she's not exactly a cat lover."

"She might do it at night," I suggested, "or in her back garden. Can you see it from here?"

We craned our necks to look out of Ellie's bedroom window. The Bird Woman lived further down the road, too far for us to see into her back garden. It was full of trees – that was all you could tell.

"Maybe we could see into it from the back alley," I said.

"The alley? It's pretty overgrown," she said doubtfully.

The alley ran along between the back gardens of Ellie's road and mine. Years ago we used it as a short cut between our houses. In those days the bin men collected rubbish from the backs of people's houses, and the alley was kept clear for them. Nowadays rubbish was collected from wheelie bins at the front. No one seemed to use the alley; it was turning into a jungle.

"That doesn't matter," I said. "In fact it's useful. She won't see us coming."

With some difficulty, we eased open Ellie's back gate and stepped into the narrow lane. Garden fences lined both sides of it, with overhanging branches well placed to smack you in the face. The ground was knee-deep in weeds, apart from a thin thread of a path running down the middle.

"Someone must still use it," I said, "or else there wouldn't be a path. Someone quite small. I know – garden gnomes use it at night to visit their friends."

"Cats, more likely." Ellie pointed down the lane to where a dark shape was just visible in the undergrowth. It poised itself, leaped up a fence with a scrabble of claws, and vanished on the other side. "This is a motorway for cats," she said, "with slip roads going off into the different gardens."

It was definitely an easier pathway for cats than for humans. We struggled along it, ducking under branches, almost tripping up in the tangled weeds. I had no idea how far we should travel, but luckily Ellie remembered to count the gates we passed.

"It's the next one," she whispered.

We crept up to the fence and peered over into the Bird Woman's back garden. It was worse than the lane – horribly overgrown. (That is, horrible by human standards. To a bird it might look like a pleasant neighbourhood, full of desirable residences.)

Squinting through the branches, we could just make out the back of the house, an untidy lawn and a couple of bird tables. It was impossible to get a good view. There might be any number of poisoned dishes set out in the undergrowth like hidden traps.

"Wouldn't she worry about poisoning birds as well as cats?" asked Ellie.

"Who knows? She's mad. She probably can't think logically. Shhh!"

There was the sound of a door being dragged open. We both instinctively ducked, although I don't know why. We had nothing to feel guilty about – anyone could walk down the alley.

Cautiously I peeped over the fence again. The Bird Woman had come out of the house. She was putting more food out on the tables; at once, birds rushed down on it with a flurry of wings. They didn't seem afraid of her at all.

She scared *me*, though. She looked exactly like an evil witch in a fairy tale. Her face seemed to have collapsed inwards, giving her a sharp, pointy nose and chin. She was bent and twisted like a stunted tree. She wore an ancient black coat and pink slippers. (OK, so witches don't wear pink slippers. But everything else was exactly right, even the way she muttered to herself as she hobbled back indoors.)

"No cat food." Ellie sounded almost disappointed. "Perhaps she doesn't put it out every day – only when the cats really annoy her."

"Or when she finds a bird that's been killed by a cat. She might think of it as a… a sort of punishment, you know?"

As I said this, I stepped backwards and trod on something squishy. No, not the sort of squishy thing you might expect… I had stepped on a cardboard plate, piled with cat food.

Yuck! Even as I frantically wiped my shoe on the grass, I realised the importance of what I'd found. The food was hidden in the tall grass, so we hadn't seen it, but any cat would know it was there by sniffing it out.

"We'd better take this to the vet," whispered Ellie.

"We need to find out if it's actually poisoned."

"Wait a minute. If we take the whole plate, she might notice"

"So?"

"She might know she's been found out. She'd stop putting food here and find somewhere else. Then we'd never be able to prove it was her."

We looked at each other. "What should we do? We can't leave the food here. It's dangerous," said Ellie.

"Take it back to your place or mine," I said, "scrape the food off, and put the empty plate back here. She'll think the cats have eaten it."

"Good idea," said Ellie. "Your house is nearer."

My back gate was a little further along on the other side of the alley. There was only one problem – we couldn't open it. It hadn't been used in ages, and there was a blackberry bush growing up against the other side.

"Back to my place, then," said Ellie, and we started the return trek through the jungle. Ellie carried the plate carefully. It was quite flimsy, and she didn't want to spill any food for cats to find.

Two doors along, or two gates rather, I heard the sound of a lawn mower. Looking over the fence, I saw our almost-neighbour, Mr Whitely, mowing his beautiful back lawn. He got quite a shock when I opened the gate and put my head around it.

"Excuse me, Mr Whitely. Could we possibly come through your garden?" I asked. (He's quite elderly, and politeness work wonders with elderly people.) "We can't seem to get our garden gate to open."

"Of course. Feel free," he said. "But what on earth have you got there?"

"It's pet food," said Ellie, showing him.

"And we think it might be poisoned," I added. "You know – like it said in the paper?"

He looked shocked. "Dear me! Are you sure? Where did you find it?"

"In the alley – the Bird Woman put it there. At least we think so. We really need to catch her at it… actually hiding the food out there."

"I'll keep an eye out for her, if it helps at all," he offered. "I'm out in my garden all the time. What a dreadful thing to do! But then she's not right in the head – I've said so for years. They ought to put her away. A public nuisance, she is, encouraging all those birds, and then they fly into my garden here and peck up all my seeds."

As we walked up the garden, I noticed something that looked at first glance like a cat crouching in a flower bed. It was actually a wooden silhouette of a cat, with shining reflective eyes. "Is that to scare off the birds?" I asked Mr Whitely.

"Not really. It's meant to keep cats away. They're forever getting into my garden and messing on my flower beds. But then that's their nature, I suppose. You can't fight nature."

I thought to myself that he'd done a good job of fighting nature in his garden. The lawn was as smooth as a pool table. The tulips stood in neat rows, like soldiers on parade. The hedge was clipped as square as a brick wall. Beautifully neat and tidy, but it wasn't a garden you could relax in.

At my house, we tipped the cat food into a plastic bag and washed our hands thoroughly. "Do be careful," said Mum. "If it's poisonous to cats, it may not do humans much good either."

Just then Ellie's mobile rang. As she listened,

a change came over her face. When she put the phone away, I saw she was terribly upset.

"It's Casper," she said. "He's ill. Mum thinks he's been poisoned – like the others."

Chapter Twelve

Nine lives

Ellie rushed back to her place. I hurried after her, but I couldn't keep up. By the time I got there, Ellie and her mum were getting into the car, taking Casper to the vet.

"Here – take this too," I gasped, shoving the bag of cat food into Ellie's hand. "It might help the vet to know what's wrong with Casper."

She took it, but I don't know if she actually heard me. All her attention was on the cat basket held tenderly on her knees.

"I do hope he's OK," I said.

She didn't answer. Her mum started the car, and they shot down the road like an ambulance racing to a motorway pile-up.

I am not a cat person, as I said before. All the same, I knew how Ellie felt about her cat – he was like part of the family. If Casper died…

I sent up silent prayers. Oh, don't let him die – please, please, please.

Late in the afternoon, Ellie rang me. "He's still alive," she said, "but the vet doesn't know if he'll make it through the night. They're keeping him at the clinic. Oh Phoebe! This is all my fault!"

"*Your* fault? Don't be stupid. How could it be your fault?"

"I should have kept him indoors, I should have looked after him better…"

"Rubbish," I said firmly. "Listen, you didn't even know about the poison until I showed you the paper.

That was only this morning, remember? By that time he'd probably eaten the stuff already."

This didn't seem to comfort her. She kept going on about how she should have known... after we found that cat in the park she should have been more careful. I could tell she was getting herself into a state.

I said, "Ellie, do you know what my mum always says? You can't change what's already happened, so it's no good worrying about it. But you can change what's *going* to happen."

"How?"

"By praying about it." I tried to sound more confident than I actually felt. "I've been praying for Casper already. You can, too."

"I don't know how," she said. "Will you say one for me? Say it now, so I can hear."

So I said a prayer for Casper over the phone, and silently added an extra bit. Please do it, God – or Ellie will think that praying is a total waste of time. (And so will I.)

Next morning Georgie shook me awake at the unearthly hour of ten-thirty.

"Go away," I muttered. "It's the holidays. I'm having a lie-in."

"But Ellie's on the phone. She said it's urgent."

My stomach lurched. It was bad news – somehow I just knew it. Reluctantly I picked up the phone. I was so sleepy and Ellie was talking so fast that for a minute I didn't take in what she was saying.

"Casper's OK! He's going to be all right! The vet says he can come home. We're just going to pick him up now."

"Oh, Ellie! That's great." I felt weak with relief.

"The vet says Casper got better much quicker than any of the other cats. It's amazing! Mum thinks he can't have eaten much of the poison. But that's not the real reason, is it? Say another prayer for me, Phoebe. Say thank you."

"Sure. But why don't you say it yourself?"

"OK. I will."

I asked her if she'd given the cat food to the vet.

"Yes, and he's sent it to be analysed. It will take a few days, he said. I told him all about finding it. But he doesn't believe the Bird Woman did it. He knows her because she sometimes takes injured birds to him. He says she's a lot nicer than she looks."

"Huh! He might think differently if he saw her like I did, with a gun in her hand."

Suddenly I remembered something. In all the fuss about Casper, I'd clean forgotten to replace the empty dish in the alley. When I asked Mum what had happened to it, she looked blank. "Did you want to keep it? Whatever for? I'm sorry, but I put it in the bin."

Holding my breath for more than one reason, I rummaged through the dustbin. Greasy chicken bones... rotten bananas... potato peelings... yuck. (Maybe I should do this every day to put me off my food.) When I found the cardboard plate, soggy, crumpled and stained with baked beans, I saw it was no use. Even a crazy woman would realise it had not been sitting quietly in the alley where she left it.

But Mum had a bright idea. "They sell plates exactly like it in the corner shop. They've got cat food, too."

I hurried down to the shop. It occurred to me that I could do some detective work, so I asked the owner if the Bird Woman had ever bought plates like that, or tins of cat food. He couldn't remember. (This sort of thing never happens to Sherlock Holmes. Why not?)

Back at home I put some cat food on a dish and scraped most of it off again. It looked good. (No, not good to eat. I mean it looked identical to the other one.) As I still couldn't get our back gate open, I went round by way of Mr Whitely's garden. He told me he'd been keeping an eye on the alley whenever he was working at the back. But he'd seen no sign of Mrs Bruce.

Bending down, I crept out of his back gate and across the alley. I hid the new plate in the grass where I'd found the old one. For the next few days, whenever I was at home, I spent some time at my bedroom window. Hiding behind the curtain, I could look diagonally across the neighbouring gardens to the back lane. I could just make out the top of the Bird Woman's gate, but I never saw it open.

Once or twice – not too often, for fear of being seen – Ellie and I ventured out into the lane. The empty plate was still where I'd left it, looking soggy now, with snail trails over it. No more food appeared.

"Perhaps she's stopped putting poison out because the cats have stopped going into her garden," Ellie suggested. "Since that newspaper article, people have kept their pets indoors."

Casper was walking restlessly round her house, like a lion in a cramped circus cage. The cat flap was bolted shut, and even Casper hadn't yet managed to master its workings. Instead he lurked by the front door whenever he heard a key in the lock, ready to make a break for freedom.

"I wish I could explain to him," Ellie said miserably. "He doesn't understand that we're doing this to help him. And I can't tell him OK, go out, but don't take any food from strangers."

"It might be safe to let him out for an hour or two," I said. "There's no food in the alley right now — we just checked."

"Yes, but if I let him out now, I might not see him again till tomorrow morning. And what if she's put some more poison out somewhere else?"

There was no answer to that.

The bad thing about being on holiday was that there was very little chance of seeing Leo, even at a distance. Once, from the library, I saw him with some friends on skateboards, practising jumps on the steps outside. (Leo was easily the best.) Hiding behind a bookshelf, I watched them for ages until a policeman came and moved them on.

Likes and dislikes about the Easter holidays

Dislikes:
1 Not seeing Leo.
2 Eating too much, because I'm at home and the food is just sitting there, asking for it.
3 Feeling bored. (Anything I really want to do costs money which I haven't got.)

Likes:
1 Not seeing Miranda, except at church where she acts all nice.
2 Missing Maths, History, Science, German, Geography, French, RE and PHSE.
3 Even better, missing Games (Yess!)
4 Easter eggs. Even dieters can have one or two, can't they? I just love those Cadbury's Creme ones, and they're only little. No, don't tell me how many calories — I don't want to know.

Chapter Thirteen

Problem page two

I thought I was safe during the holidays — I thought Miranda couldn't hurt me. But I was wrong.

Sunday began badly. I weighed myself and found that in the week since Easter I'd gained two pounds! It must have been those Easter eggs.

"That's it. I'm giving them up," I promised Mum. "I won't touch another Easter egg for a whole year."

"It's not just the eggs, though, is it?" she said. "It's all the little snacks you've been having, crisps and cakes and things. Why don't you eat an orange or some celery sticks?"

"I often *do* eat an orange. An orange Club biscuit."

What made it even worse was the fact that Mum was losing weight. She had lost six pounds, the same as me (except that I'd put half of it back on) and she was still managing to stick to her diet. I knew I should feel pleased for her, but it was difficult.

Mum said, "At slimming club they told us to think about why we eat things. Sometimes it's nothing to do with hunger. If we overeat because we're depressed or bored, then we ought to find food-free ways to cheer ourselves up."

She was saying "we" but I knew who she meant. OK, I admit it — I do want to eat when I'm bored. Also when I am happy/lonely/depressed/excited/worried/totally indifferent. I must have an addictive personality. At least food is less harmful than alcohol or drug addiction — isn't it?

"It's probably my fault," said Mum.

Not another one! Ellie felt guilty over her cat's eating habits. Now here was Mum feeling guilty over mine.

"OK, so it's your fault," I said. "You force fed me on Cadbury's Creme Eggs. I didn't want to eat them but you made me."

"It was Smarties actually," said Mum. "You won't remember this, but when Georgie was born she was quite a delicate baby. She had trouble feeding..."

"Huh! She's made up for it since," I said.

"And she was slow to put on weight. She used to take about an hour over each feed. You were only two at the time, and of course you got bored and wanted attention. But I couldn't put Georgie down in the middle of her feed. I used to read to you, and when you got bored with that, I'd give you Smarties to keep you quiet."

I didn't remember that at all. My first clear memory was of cutting my head open at the age of four, when I fell off a swing.

Mum went on, "So you learned that if you were bored, you should get a sweet. And it's my fault."

"Georgie's fault, you mean." Typical! Before she was a year old, Georgie had managed to ruin my entire life. And she hadn't changed. She was still a selfish attention-grabber who never put on weight.

What about me? Had I changed? Could it really be true that I was stuck in a behaviour pattern I'd learned when I was two?

I talked about it to Sarah as we hung around before youth group. She thought Mum might have a point.

"Hey, I learned about this in Science," she said. "There was a famous experiment with pigeons who were trained to press a button whenever they heard a bell ring. Every time they did it, they got rewarded with bird seed."

"What's that got to do with me? It may have escaped your notice, Sarah, but I'm not a pigeon. See – no feathers. No beak."

"Just listen, will you? After a while the pigeons learned it so well that they sort of did it automatically. Even when the scientist stopped rewarding them, they still did it. Hear the bell, press the button. Hear the bell, press the button."

I said, "You mean that's what *I* do? Feel bored, eat food… feel bored, eat food?"

"Could be. I mean when I feel bad, it doesn't make me head for the biscuit tin. My mobile, or a CD, or some money to go shopping – that's what I look for. Not food."

"Shhh." Lizzie and Sam had sat down near us, and I didn't want them to hear. It was OK for Sarah to discuss my eating problems, but I didn't want the entire youth group joining in.

Things were a bit chaotic that evening because Pete, the usual leader, wasn't there. His car had broken down and he was waiting for the AA. This meant that Becky was in charge, and Becky is the world's most indecisive person.

"Oh dear," said Becky helplessly. "What should we do? I've no idea what Pete planned for this evening."

"I know what we could do," Miranda said at once. She described the Problem Page session at the school CU. Becky, being Becky, looked doubtful, but Miranda's enthusiasm swept everyone else along with her. Soon we were all writing furiously or chewing thoughtfully on our pencils.

I wrote, "Why do some prayers get answered and not others?" I was thinking of my two most recent, most urgent prayers. Casper was still alive – great! Thank you, God! And I was still fat. Great. Thanks a lot.

As I folded up my paper, I noticed Miranda doing the same. She folded hers so many times that it looked like a tiny parcel. All the time, she had a nasty smile on her face. What was she up to?

Taking charge completely, she collected all the papers and put them in a pile. "Now we choose one at random," she said. At random – sure. Her hand went straight for her own paper, the many-times-folded one. (Not that anyone else would know it was hers.)

Opening it, she read: "I have a serious weight problem. I know I look terrible and I will never get a boyfriend, but I can't seem to stop eating. What should I do?"

Twenty pairs of eyes homed in on me, then hastily looked away. After all, I was the fattest person in the room; I was also pink with embarrassment. Of course they all assumed that I'd written the question. Miranda had done it again... made people notice me for all the wrong reasons.

I couldn't bear it. I simply could not sit there while people tried, ever so tactfully and without naming names, to talk about Fat Phoebe and her problems.

Standing up with as much dignity as I could scrape together, I said coldly, "I don't know why you're all looking at me. I didn't write that question – Miranda did. If she thinks she's overweight, I'd say she's got a serious self-image problem." Then I walked straight out of the room and out of the building.

Behind me I heard the sound of feet running to catch up. It was Sarah.

"Are you OK?" She took my arm. "I can't believe Miranda did that. What an absolute *cow* she is. But you handled it really well."

I felt slightly comforted. "I'm not going back in there," I said.

"I don't blame you. I'll walk home with you if you like."

As we walked, I told her all about Miranda's hate campaign. Sarah was totally on my side. "I remember she was pretty foul to you at my birthday meal," she said. "She's horrible. Why does she do it?"

"You know what I think? It's like you were saying earlier. When I feel bad I eat things. When you feel bad you go shopping. But Miranda... when she feels bad she tries to make someone else feel even worse. That's what she does. Somehow it cheers her up."

Sarah asked if I had told my parents. I shook my head. "What's the point? What could they do?"

"They could talk to Miranda's mum."

"Yeah, if they could get a word in edgeways. But Mum wouldn't want to – she hates making trouble."

Dad might do it, though. He was more assertive than Mum. I decided to tell him as soon as possible.

Sarah said gloomily, "Miranda's supposed to be staying with me next weekend. I wish she wasn't."

"Can't you get out of it?"

"Not really. Her parents are going to some kind of church conference, so they fixed up for Miranda to sleep over at my place. I'll just have to hope she gets flu or something."

"Or double pneumonia," I said hopefully. "Or leprosy."

"Meningitis."

"Hepatitis."

"Mad cow disease."

"Ingrown toenails."

In the end I did tell Mum and Dad what had happened. To my surprise, they both took it seriously. Even Mum was prepared to take action. She tried to ring Miranda's parents, but no one was in.

"I'll try again tomorrow," she promised.

But it didn't do any good. Somehow I knew it wouldn't.

Mum said, "You know what Mary Frost is like – she can talk the hind leg off a donkey. I don't think she really listened to me. Whatever I said, she stood up for Miranda. 'Oh, I'm sure she would never say anything deliberately cruel, she's not that sort of person. Perhaps Miranda made a little joke and Phoebe took it the wrong way. Could it be that Phoebe is a touch oversensitive?'"

This made me really angry. Miranda must have got to her mother first with her side of the story – and of course her mum believed every word.

"So then, I'm afraid, I got quite cross," said Mum. Dad and I both looked at her, startled.

"I told Mary that she's foolish if she thinks Miranda can do no wrong. I said Miranda's not perfect – she has her faults, just like everyone else. And then, luckily, Mary put the phone down on me. Because I was just about to say something really nasty."

"Like what?" I asked.

"Like mentioning Martin."

Dad understood this, but I didn't. "Who's Martin?"

Dad said, "I don't suppose you remember him. He was Miranda's brother, but a lot older than her. Ten years older? Anyway, he got in with a bad crowd in his teenage years. Drug-taking, stealing – he stole from his own parents."

"In the end he ran away from home," said Mum. "No one knows where he is now; they don't know if he's alive or dead."

"I didn't realise she had a brother," I said. "She never talks about him."

Dad said, "She would only have been about five when he left home. She probably doesn't miss him. But you can understand, can't you, what it did to her parents..."

"It broke Mary's heart," said Mum.

"Yes, and it made her very protective about Miranda," said Dad. "She's determined that Miranda won't end up like Martin."

"So that's why she treats Miranda like a little kid," I said, remembering the night of Sarah's birthday. Just for a second I felt sorry for Miranda. It wasn't her fault that her brother had gone off the rails... but now, to make up for it, her parents wanted her to be a good little girl, 100 per cent perfect.

"The sad thing is," said Mum, "it won't do Miranda any good in the long run."

No. And it wouldn't do me any good, either. Because tomorrow I had to go back to school and face Miranda.

Chapter Fourteen

Out of order

"Mum, I forgot – I need my tennis things for tomorrow."

"*Now* she tells me," Mum said rather crossly. She was in the middle of putting Josh to bed. "Have a look in the second drawer down."

I looked. Surely that wasn't the tennis skirt I'd worn last summer? It seemed far too tight and too short. I struggled into it, just managing to fasten the zip. When I saw myself in the mirror, I wanted to cry.

"You look like a tennis-playing hippo," said my kind sister.

"Shut up! Mum! I can't wear this! I need a new one."

"And where do you suppose I can get a tennis skirt from at this time of night?" Mum said.

"But I *can't* wear this. Could you write a note to get me out of Games? Say I've hurt my foot or something." Even as I said it, I knew the answer would be no. Mum hates telling lies.

"You'll have to use your winter Games kit," she said calmly.

I didn't argue, because I'd already decided what to do. I would simply hide in the toilets for the entire Games lesson. The end toilet didn't work; it had an OUT OF ORDER sign on the door, which was locked shut. But I'd discovered how to unlock it from the outside. It was easy – all you needed was a nail file to use like a screwdriver.

I had to work quickly while there was no one else in the room. When I was inside the cubicle, I locked the door again. Just in time – I heard footsteps and voices, familiar voices. Miranda was out there with her friends; they were probably preening themselves in front of the mirror. (Staying beautiful must be such hard work.)

"So are we really going ahead with it?" asked Lauren in a low voice.

"Of course we are," said Miranda. "At least I am. Anyone want to chicken out?"

Jade said, "But what would your parents say if they found out? They'd ground you for absolutely years."

"It would be worth it," Miranda said defiantly. "But don't worry. They won't find out."

What on earth were they talking about? Trying to hear better, I held my ear to the door – which was a mistake. Thud! Clang! Thud! Clang! Someone was kicking all the toilet doors open, making sure there were no hidden listeners. The noise made my head ring like a bell.

"My mum and dad will be in Manchester on Saturday. They're leaving at six in the morning," said Miranda. "I'm supposed to be going to stay with this girl called Sarah, but she has ballet class in the morning, so her mum will pick me up at lunch time. Or so my parents think." She laughed.

"How are you going to get out of it?" asked Jade.

"I'll ring Sarah's family to say I'm ill. What I mean is, my mum will ring them." Miranda's voice changed suddenly. In a good imitation of her mother's non-stop flow of chatter, she said, "I'm *so* sorry, but Miranda's a tiny bit under the weather. Sore throat, sneezing, feverish – I'm afraid she may have flu. So I've decided to give the conference a miss and stay at home to look after her. It's such a pity – but these things are sent to try us. I do hope poor Sarah won't be too disappointed."

The others laughed.

"Excellent," said Lauren. "So then we'll have the rest of the day to get ready."

"What do we need?" asked Jade. "Drinks of course. Food?"

Miranda said, "No food – it's too messy. Don't forget I've got to clean up afterwards. But what about music?"

By now I'd guessed they were planning a party – the kind of party Miranda's mum wouldn't allow in a million years. And it sounded as if... no, surely not. Surely they weren't intending to have it at Miranda's house?

I didn't hear any more, because at that moment Miss Marne came barging in, rounding up stragglers. "What are you girls doing in here? You should have been outside ten minutes ago. Get a move on!" Thud, clang, thud, clang, louder than before, as she kick-boxed her way along the row of toilets. She even kicked my door, despite the OUT OF ORDER sign. (I've always suspected that Games teachers are illiterate.)

After they had gone the room settled into peaceful stillness, apart from the slow drip of a tap. But my thoughts weren't at all peaceful. If only I knew how to contact Miranda's parents in Manchester! I could send them a message that would make them hurry home, to find Miranda's party in full swing... Miranda drunk as a skunk... Miranda snogging some boy she'd only just met...

She would be in horrendous trouble, but she fully deserved it. Her parents would be shocked to learn the truth about her – they deserved that, too. One phone call was all it would take. What a pity I had no way of knowing their number.

Don't ask me what the CU meeting was about. I sat through it without hearing a word, my mind was so busy.

But at the end I saw something that brought me back to reality.

Miranda was talking to Leo. She wrote something on a page of her work book, tore it out and gave it to him. Her address, her phone number? Oh... suddenly I knew. She was telling him about the party.

Say no, Leo! Tell her you're busy! It's going to be a lousy party, I can guarantee it. No skateboards for one thing...

But he was nodding and smiling. He put the folded paper in his pocket; then he hurried out. Miranda came towards me, her face full of triumph. She looked as if she'd won the London Marathon, *Blind Date* and the National Lottery, all in one day.

She whispered, "Phoebe, I just *had* to tell you. Leo's coming to my party!"

"Is he?" I kept my voice quite level. "That's nice. I do hope he likes Pass the Parcel and Pin the Tail on the Donkey."

She hissed, "Don't be stupid. It's not that kind of party."

"I don't believe you – your mum will never let you have a proper party. In fact, I bet she's busy right now making pink jelly and a birthday cake with six candles on the top."

"It *is* a proper party," she snapped. "And for your information, my parents won't even –" Then all at once she fell silent, like a cut-off phone.

"Yes?" I said sweetly.

Miranda, for once, had nothing to say. She turned and stalked out of the room.

Ellie stared after her. "What was all that about, then?" I told her of my suspicions, and tried to explain what Miranda's mother was like.

"They must be mad," she gasped. "They'll never get away with it. No matter how carefully they tidy up afterwards, I bet Miranda's parents notice something."

I put on a Miranda's-mother voice. "Darling, how on earth do you suppose all these empty bottles got into our dustbin? 62 Bacardi Breezers and 37 beer cans? It's very strange. And the neighbours have complained about loud music on Saturday night. Well, it *can't* have come from our house, I told them. We were all away. Miranda? Where are you going?"

Ellie said, "Maybe they're planning on keeping it quite low key. A small select group, just the four of them and whatever boys they've got their eyes on."

And Miranda had invited Leo. I felt sick at the thought. Leo and Miranda talking, dancing together, kissing... He might quite easily fall for her. She was attractive and confident, and when it suited her she could be nice – no one would guess how poisonous she really was. Not until it was too late.

I hated the idea of Leo getting involved with her. But what could I do? If I tried to tell him what she was like, he'd think I was simply jealous. He wouldn't listen. Oh, if only there was some way of putting a stop to that party...

By now we were hurrying towards a double Maths lesson (oh, what fun). Further along the corridor was a large, slow-moving shape, a bit like a furniture truck blocking a country lane. It was Smurf, Miranda's secret stalker.

The idea came quite suddenly in a burst of brilliance. Sheer genius! Before I had time to think about it, I hurried after Smurf. Overtaking him was not hard, even for someone athletically challenged like me.

"Hold on a minute. I've got a message for you," I said to him.

He came slowly to a halt. An expression of surprise crept gradually onto his big, spotty face, like a cloud shadow moving across a mountain.

"You what?" he said.

"A message. From Miranda Frost. She's having a party and she wants you to go."

"Does she?" He looked pleased for a second, then suspicious. Perhaps he wasn't quite as stupid as I'd thought; I would have to do a bit of persuading.

I said, "You know she likes you. But she has to pretend not to care about you because of her parents. They're dead strict – they'd go mad if they found out she talked to you. So that's why she got me to pass on the message. She said be sure to mention that her parents won't be around."

He smiled – not a pretty sight. He had teeth like a Roman ruin. "So when is this party?"

"Saturday night at Miranda's place – 47 Nightingale Lane."

"Yeah, yeah, I know where she lives," he said. "Tell her I'll be there."

I became conscious of fingers digging into my arm. It was Ellie, looking as if she wanted to say something, but I ignored her.

"Bring some drinks," I told him, adding recklessly, "and tell all your friends." If he had any friends, which was doubtful. He nodded eagerly, like one of those brainless toy dogs in the back of a car.

"Got to go now. I've got Maths." And I hurried off, managing to keep a straight face until I was around the corner.

"Oh, Phoebe," said Ellie, "I don't think you should have done that."

"Why ever not?" I said, surprised. "Don't you think Miranda deserves everything she gets?"

"That's not what I meant. I thought Christians aren't supposed to…" Her voice tailed off.

"Supposed to what?"

"Oh nothing."

She wouldn't say any more. But I could sort of guess what she was thinking. Christians aren't supposed to tell lies. Or stir up trouble. Or take revenge on people.

Maybe she had a point. Maybe I shouldn't have done it. But I didn't care. I was quite looking forward to Saturday night.

Chapter Fifteen

The old dark house

Next evening Ellie rang me, full of excitement. "I just had a phone call from Michael Welch," she said.

"Michael who?"

"You know – the vet," she said impatiently. "Remember he sent that cat food off to be tested? He's just got the results back. It *was* poisoned."

"Has he told the police?"

"He phoned the RSPCA. He says if there's any evidence against whoever put the food out, the RSPCA could prosecute them. But it wouldn't be easy to prove. I mean, anyone can go down that alley. We've got no actual evidence against the Bird Woman."

"We ought to take another look," I said.

It was several days since we'd visited the back alley. The nettles seemed to have grown even taller; the long grass felt damp against my legs. And it was a wasted journey. No new food had been put out. The old cardboard plate was starting to fall apart.

"Did you ask the vet if any more cats have been poisoned?" I asked, or rather whispered. (I don't know why I was whispering. Somehow the alley, deserted and overgrown, seemed a secretive sort of place.)

Ellie said, "After Casper, nothing happened for a couple of weeks. But then yesterday some people brought in a stray that they'd found being sick in their garden. It had exactly the same symptoms. It died this morning."

"So she's still doing it!" I looked over the fence at the

jungle-like garden, shadowy in the dusk.

"What's that over there?" said Ellie, pointing. Something was wedged in the fork of a tree close to the house. A brown china bowl, it looked like. From where we stood, we couldn't see what it might contain.

"I'm going in there," Ellie said in a don't-try-and-stop-me voice.

"But she might see you!"

"What if she does? You think she'll put an evil spell on me, or something?"

Well no, not exactly. But I did feel quite scared of the old woman – she looked so weird. And I hadn't forgotten the gun...

There was a gate in the fence. Ellie leaned over and tried to undo the bolt on the far side, but she couldn't. "It's all rusty," she said. "Looks like it hasn't been opened in years. I'll have to climb over."

"Oh, be careful," I said, feeling helpless. There was no way I could get past that fence, not without the aid of a bulldozer. But Ellie, long-legged and agile, might manage it.

The fence creaked ominously as she swung herself up and over. Nothing broke, though. She jumped down into the nettles with a muffled yelp of pain. I looked anxiously towards the house, where two black windows seemed to gaze at us like the empty eyes of a blind man.

"Wait a minute," Ellie whispered. "I'll have another go at that gate." She leant all her weight against it and managed to shift the rusty bolt and heave the gate open. Oh, terrific. Now I had to pretend to be brave like Ellie.

And something was bothering me. If that gate hadn't been opened in ages, then how could –

"Come on," Ellie whispered.

We fought our way through the bushes, with dried

twigs cracking underfoot, loud as gunshots. At last we reached the straggly lawn. Still there was no sign of movement in the silent, brooding house. No lights had come on, though by now it was nearly dark.

The bowl in the tree held nothing but a small amount of water. "A bird bath," said Ellie, disappointed. "But we may as well have a look around while we're here."

There was nothing to see except two bird tables, a broken clothes line and an old, rotting bench.

"Let's get out of here," I muttered.

"Shhh! What's that? Look – by the door."

I suddenly realised that the back door was open just a crack. And something had come through the gap. Something pale and thin was lying on the doorstep. It looked like… a hand.

My stomach lurched. I stared at the thing, the white, gnarled, ancient hand. I saw it move feebly, then lie still.

"It's her," Ellie gasped. "She's in there!"

I wanted to run away. But somehow I couldn't. That hand, so helpless, reaching out to us…

"Maybe she's ill," I said.

"Maybe she's *dead*."

We crept closer. "Mrs Bruce?" I said nervously. "Are you all right?"

No answer. I tried to push the door open, but it wouldn't move. She must have fallen so that her body was blocking the doorway.

"We'd better call an ambulance," I said, getting my mobile out.

"And I'll call my mum," said Ellie.

A couple of minutes later her mum, Jackie, came running down the alley. I was really glad to see her. It hadn't been nice, just Ellie and me in the chill twilight, possibly with a dead body around the corner.

Even with Jackie's help, we couldn't push the back door any further open. "I wonder if we can get in any other way?" she said.

Luckily the front door was unlocked. Jackie groped her way into the dark hallway and felt around for a light switch. Just then I heard the siren of the ambulance; I ran out to flag it down.

The paramedics quickly took control. They told us Mrs Bruce was still alive, but unconscious – perhaps she'd had a stroke. Soon they were carrying her out to the ambulance. "What a good thing you found her," one of them said. "If she'd had to lie there in the cold all night, well…" She might have died, I suppose he meant.

"Are you neighbours of hers?" the other one asked. "Do you think you could make sure the house is locked up?"

"Of course," said Jackie.

We watched as the flashing blue light disappeared into the dusk. "Poor old dear," said Jackie. "All alone with nobody to help her."

"Doesn't she have any family?" I asked.

"I don't think so. Her husband died years ago, and after that she sort of cut herself off from people. The only things she cared about were her birds."

"And *they* weren't much help when she needed them," I said.

Ellie snorted. "She wasn't a poor old dear. She was an old witch who poisoned cats. And I bet we can find the proof of it right here in this house."

"Ellie!" said her mother, shocked. "You can't go digging around in someone else's house."

But in the end we had to go digging around, because we couldn't find a key to lock the front door.

"She must have hidden it somewhere." Jackie gazed

around the cluttered hallway, where junk mail lay unopened in a heap, and a row of frayed black coats hung like sleeping vampire bats. "Goodness knows where. It would take a week to search this place properly."

"I'll look in the kitchen," said Ellie, and I followed her.

The kitchen cupboards held stacks of old crockery, furry with dust. There was very little food. The old lady must have lived on bread, margarine and cornflakes. (And possibly bird food – there was plenty of that.)

Ellie said, "I was hoping we might find some tins of Kit-e-Kat. But hey – look at this!" She snatched something out of the sink.

"The gun!" I cried.

Ellie began to laugh. "Sure – the gun. Here, have a closer look."

I felt a total idiot. It wasn't a gun; it was a plastic water pistol. Annoyed, I squirted her in the face, and she leapt away – just like the cat had done that night.

"Well, it *was* pretty dark at the time," I said defensively.

Perhaps the Bird Woman wasn't a killer at all. A squirt of water would not hurt cats, but it might make them think twice about visiting her garden.

And her garden gate had been rusted solid. So she couldn't have been the person who put the cat food out in the alley... not unless she climbed over the fence or walked all the way to the end of the road. Somehow we'd got it all wrong. But if the Bird Woman hadn't been poisoning cats – who had?

"Found the key!" Jackie called. "It was under the doormat."

"Let's go," said Ellie, shivering slightly. "I don't like this place – it's scary."

Strangely enough, the dark old house didn't scare me, not any more. Nor did the Bird Woman. She wasn't a gun-crazy cat-killing lunatic – just a lonely old lady. And now she was ill in hospital, cut off from the only creatures she cared about.

I decided I would feed the birds and visit her in hospital, to reassure her they were surviving without her.

Chapter Sixteen

Party night

On Saturday Ellie and I went to the cinema with a couple of mates. It was a slushy romantic comedy. You know – girl meets boy, hates him at first, but later discovers he's Mr Wonderful.

I thought of Miranda getting ready for her party, putting on make-up, jewellery and perfume… all for Leo's benefit. Meanwhile Smurf would be brushing his misshapen teeth, trying to cover up his spots… all for Miranda. And I grinned to myself. Would Smurf turn out to be Miranda's Mr Wonderful? I felt the odds were against it.

We went home on the bus. As we passed the park in the gathering dusk, I noticed a group of boys hanging around the shelter. I was almost sure that Smurf was one of them – he towered over the others like a heavyweight boxer.

Q Why would a gang of Year 9 boys visit the park after nightfall?

1 To study the nocturnal wildlife (bats, owls and snogging couples).

2 To chuck a supermarket trolley in the pond.

3 To avoid the long walk to the public loos.

4 To drink Extra Strong lager.

A:4, at least I hoped so. (They could do the other things

as well if they liked.)

If Smurf and his friends arrived at the party drunk, the result could be chaos. I longed to see it – if only Miranda lived closer to me! But of course there was always the phone...

I gave the party some time to get going. At around nine-thirty I rang the house; I heard Miranda telling someone to turn down the music. Then she said hello, and I put the phone down hurriedly.

I waited half an hour, then rang again. This time it was Jade who picked up the phone. Acting on impulse, I asked if I could speak to Mrs Frost. "It's Fran Wilson," I said.

"Who?"

"Fran Wilson, from church. My, that sounds like quite a party you're having."

"Er... hold on a minute." Jade went away, probably to ask Miranda how to deal with this. Then, through the thumping music, I heard a doorbell ring.

Amazing! I couldn't have timed it better. Smurf and his friends were on the doorstep. (The phone must have been in the hallway – I could hear everything.)

"Oh, it's you." Miranda's voice was far from welcoming. "What do you want?"

"Heard you were having a party," said Smurf. "And we couldn't miss that, could we guys?"

"But you're not invited. So get lost, all of you." I pictured her trying to shut the door. Not easy, if Smurf's size 13 foot was in the way.

Smurf said, "You did invite me. And you said to bring my friends."

"No, I didn't!" Her voice had risen about an octave. "Stop that! You can't come in!" Too late. Judging by the sound of feet, they were in.

"Now, that's not very nice, is it?" Smurf was slurring

his words a bit — he had definitely had a drink or two. "You got what's-her-name... Fifi? Bibi?... to give me a message. Party Saturday, mum and dad not there, know what I mean? Then you tell me go away. What's matter with you, eh?"

"I don't know what you're talking about. If you don't get out NOW I'm calling the police."

Someone laughed. "See, I told you — she does this all the time. Pretends to like people, then turns round and kicks them in the teeth." The voice was bitter.

It sounded like Harry Price, a boy in my form. A few months ago there had been rumours about him and Miranda... I really hoped Leo was hearing this.

"Won't be like that with me," said Smurf with drunken confidence. "Miranda loves me, I know she does. C'mere, Miranda."

"Get off. Take your hands off me!" Her voice became a scream. "Leo! Help me!"

"Let go of her. Did you hear me?" It was Leo's voice. He sounded quite calm and cool.

There was a second's pause. I imagined Smurf looking round slowly, and taking in the situation even more slowly. "Oh yeah?" he said at last. "You going to make me?"

"If I have to."

Smurf said, "Is she going out with you?"

"No, but..."

"Then it's none of your business. Get lost."

"I said, leave her alone."

Smurf's friends began chanting, "Fight! Fight! Fight!" I heard confused noises, a scream, a crash... Then the line went dead. The phone must have been pulled out of its socket.

I began to feel scared. If Leo and Smurf were fighting,

I wouldn't place any bets on Leo. He was a year older, but Smurf was bigger, heavier, angrier and drunk. Oh help… I didn't mean this to happen, I really didn't.

What could I do? Maybe I ought to tell Dad, get him to go round there… But he would wonder how I got involved. It might all come out – the fact that it was my fault Smurf was there.

Should I phone the police? I could pretend to be a neighbour of Miranda's, worried by the noise of fighting. But what could I say when they asked for my name?

I tried ringing Miranda's place again and got the engaged tone. Perhaps she was calling the police – or an ambulance.

In the end I did nothing at all. I went to bed, but I couldn't sleep.

Next day Sarah was waiting for me outside church, looking excited.

"You'll never guess what Miranda's done!" she whispered. "You know she was supposed to be staying with us while her parents were away? She never came. She had a party at her place! And some gatecrashers got in and started a fight…"

I tried to look surprised and shocked.

"So Miranda got panicky and rang us, and Dad went round. It was all over when he got there, but one boy had to go to hospital. And the place was a mess. And Miranda's parents had to come back from Manchester at midnight! I wish I could see their faces."

"The boy who got hurt – who was he?" I said urgently.

"I don't know. He fell on some broken glass – blood everywhere, but Dad said it wasn't too serious. He would need a few stitches, that's all."

I felt a tiny bit better. At least Leo (if it was Leo)

hadn't been beaten to a pulp. At least I wouldn't have *that* on my conscience.

Sarah gave me an odd sort of look. "What's the matter? I thought you would be pleased to hear about Miranda getting into trouble."

"I am," I said, but it wasn't true. Which was strange. My list of wishes had all come true. (Ting! You *shall* go to the ball!) Miranda was in deep trouble, her party ruined, her parents furious. I should be feeling terrific. Instead I felt as if a beautiful gift-wrapped present had turned out to contain a dead rat.

The church service didn't help. The Bible reading was about Jesus talking to the Pharisees – the super-religious people who thought God was pleased with them.

'How terrible for you Pharisees! You clean the outside of your cup and plate, while the inside is full of violence and selfishness.'

I knew what that meant. It meant pretending to be a good little Christian, saying the right things in church and CU, outwardly keeping the rules... while all the time being bad on the inside. Hating people. Trying to hurt them. I had accused Miranda of that – but I was just the same.

I felt really depressed. Mum noticed and asked what was wrong, but I couldn't tell her.

In the afternoon I offered to take Josh out in his buggy. Maybe if I did a few good deeds, they would cancel out the bad things I'd done, and make me feel better... It didn't work, though. I bought a king size Yorkie bar, gave Josh a piece and ate the rest. That didn't work either.

Then, as I rounded a corner, a skateboarder almost collided with the buggy. It was Leo! My heart jumped like a skateboard hitting a kerb.

"Sorry," he said. "Oh – hi, Phoebe."

Surprise and embarrassment made me stammer like an idiot. "But I thought – weren't you – I heard you were in hospital. Are you OK?"

He said, "It wasn't me that ended up in hospital, it was Smurf. He cut his hand open."

That figured; Smurf was always accident prone. He should have been a deckhand on the *Titanic*.

I said, "Smurf! That guy's a total idiot. He's got a brain the size of a dried pea." I saw from Leo's face that he didn't like this remark. Trying to explain it, I blundered on. "I mean he must be crazy to think Miranda fancied him!"

Leo gave me a long, hard stare. "Yes," he said coldly. "What on earth could have given him that idea?" Then, without waiting for an answer, he stepped on his board and shot away.

"Bye-bye," said Josh. "Bye-bye."

Chapter Seventeen

Rear window

I walked home very slowly. Josh's buggy was not normally hard to push, but now it seemed to weigh about a ton. Or maybe that was the weight of my misery.

How did Leo know what I'd done? Smurf hadn't said my name – not properly. But Leo could have put two and two together. Had he told Miranda?

And another thing – I shouldn't have made that comment about Smurf's pea-sized brain. Leo hated anything like that. ("You know what a bit of a joke can do to people? It can kill them.") Smurf might look and act like a cave troll from *Lord of the Rings*, but to Leo he was still a human being with feelings.

The thought chilled me like a winter wind – Leo was right. On my scale of A to F for boys, Smurf rated Z. But he was still a person, not a thing. I had used him like a weapon, to hurt Miranda with and throw away afterwards.

I never once considered what it would do to him. Raising his hopes, then smashing them to bits... making people laugh at him... hearing he was in hospital, and being pleased it was him, not Leo... It was worse than anything Miranda had done to me.

Miranda wasn't in school next day. Nor was Smurf. And all kinds of mad rumours circulated, getting wilder with each telling. Miranda had held a drunken orgy. Her house had caught fire and burnt to the ground. Smurf had tried to slit his wrists... and so on and so on.

Miranda's friends were in school, but they weren't talking to anyone. They went round in a tight little group, ignoring all questions about the party. I passed Leo in the corridor once, but I kept my head down. I don't know if he saw me.

Within a few days Mum and Dad had heard the story too. (The church prayer network must be almost as efficient as the Year 9 gossip channel.) They had heard that Miranda's parents were furious, blaming her school friends for leading her astray. They planned to transfer her to St Margaret's, the private school where Sarah went. "Which will cost them an arm and a leg," said Dad.

"I think they're overreacting," said Mum. "Changing schools isn't the answer. It will be so disruptive for Miranda – she may not find it easy to make friends. What do you think, Phoebe?"

I muttered something. Actually it was the best news I'd heard in weeks. Yes, change schools, and while you're at it, change churches too. Or why not move to Australia?

Smurf came back to school with his right hand bandaged, which made it impossible to write, or so he claimed. (Few of the teachers had noticed he was left-handed.) I thought he might ask me some awkward questions, but he said nothing. Perhaps he thought I was quite innocent – I'd simply delivered Miranda's message as she asked me to. Perhaps he wanted to forget the whole thing.

I wished I could do that. But I still felt awful.

To take my mind off things, I suggested to Ellie that we should feed the Bird Woman's birds for her. Ellie didn't look too keen, but her mum said, "What a good idea. There was plenty of bird seed in her kitchen, wasn't there? We've still got the house key."

"Come with us, Mum," Ellie begged. "I hate that place – it's creepy."

With difficulty, we got out of Ellie's house while keeping Casper inside. "Oh, poor thing, he's getting really fed up," said Jackie. "But we can't risk letting him out. Did you see this week's paper?"

I nodded. Another cat had died at the weekend. (This was definite proof that the Bird Woman was innocent – she had been in hospital since last Wednesday.)

It was a warm evening, but the old house felt chilly inside. And there was a sickly smell, which Jackie traced to some ancient milk in the fridge. "Go on, feed the birds," she said. "I'll have a bit of a clear out in here."

Ellie took some bird seed into the back garden; I began to fill a jug with water for the bird bath. Suddenly Ellie was back indoors.

"I've just seen something odd," she whispered. "Tell me I didn't imagine it." She pulled me towards the kitchen window. I couldn't see anything except trees, bushes and long evening shadows.

"What is it?"

"You can't see from here, the trees are in the way," she said. "But if we go outside again he might notice us... Come upstairs."

She led me into a back bedroom, where bare floorboards creaked beneath our feet. We peered round the edge of a moth-eaten curtain. I could see the untidy garden and the alley beyond, then Mr Whitely's neat lawns, and – what on earth was Mr Whitely doing?

He was climbing in through an upstairs window. Somehow he looked furtive, as if he was burgling his own home. When he got inside he turned and looked out in all directions, checking he hadn't been seen. Ellie and I shrank back behind the curtain.

"I saw him climb out on that flat roof bit," said Ellie.

"So? It's his house. He can climb about on the roof if he wants to."

"Yes, but see what he was carrying. He put it down on the roof – there, in the corner. What does that look like to you?"

From this distance it was hard to be sure, but certainly it looked like... a bowl of cat food.

I said, "He doesn't like cats. He said they get into his garden and mess on his flower beds, remember?"

We stared at each other. "It's him!" Ellie breathed.

"First of all he put the poison in the alley," I said, thinking aloud. "But we found that and started keeping a lookout. So he thought it would be safer on the roof. Cats go up on those flat roofs all the time."

"No one would see it except from here," said Ellie. "The Bird Woman didn't notice, or didn't care."

I could hardly believe it. "I thought he was helping us. I mean, he seemed... he just seemed like a friendly old guy. Not a poisoner."

"You can't judge by appearances," Ellie said darkly. "Come on – let's tell Mum."

The problem was, we needed evidence. We had to get hold of that cat food so that the vet could test it. After all it's not a crime to put cat food on your roof.

Jackie – who loves cats as much as Ellie does – wanted to take action before some other poor animal had to suffer. She was sure she could get up on the flat roof with the help of a ladder. But how could we get a ladder along the alley and into the garden without being seen? It would have to be done while Mr Whitely was in his front garden.

"He often works out there in the evening," I said.

"I could keep watch, and call you when it's all clear."

"Good idea," said Jackie.

I hurried home, slowing to a saunter when I saw the top of Mr Whitely's bald head. We were in luck — he was leaning on the front garden wall, chatting to a neighbour. What a nice, kind old man, always smiling...

From our front porch I kept an eye on him, while phoning Ellie. "Get in there, quick," I said. "I don't know how long we've got."

The neighbour moved on. Mr Whitely got to work, raking and weeding. After a few minutes I rang Ellie again. "Don't keep ringing," she said crossly. "We're half way down the alley. Ever tried carrying a ladder through the Amazon jungle?"

"Can't say I have. But I did take an ironing board to the North Pole once."

"Oh shut up. This isn't funny."

I looked out cautiously. The shadows were lengthening. How long before Mr Whitely went to put his tools away in the shed around the back? I felt so nervous, I could hardly stand still. Surely they must be in the garden by now, setting the ladder up, starting the climb...

I was getting hungry. I also needed the loo. This surveillance work was much harder than it looked on TV, and more monotonous. Why didn't I get to do the exciting bit? (Answer — because I would probably break the ladder or fall through the flat roof.)

Suddenly I jerked to attention. Mr Whitely had started to gather up his gardening tools. My fingers jabbed at the buttons of my phone. "Quick!" I gasped. "He'll be round there in a minute."

"Oh — but Mum's still up on the roof!"

Help, help... I had to stall him — I had to give Jackie

more time. Hurrying down our path, I called out, "Mr Whitely. Wait!"

It was one of the many times when I've longed to be quicker on my feet. Just as I reached his gate, he disappeared round the side of the house. A moment later, I heard his furious roar.

"Hey, you! What d'you think you're doing on my roof?"

Chapter Eighteen

Coming home

I ran round the side of the house. Jackie was at the top of the ladder; Mr Whitely stood at the bottom, looking angry enough to kick it away from under her feet.

"Get down here!" he yelled.

Jackie climbed down, taking her time. When she stood on level ground she was as tall as Mr Whitely and just as angry. She was holding a plastic bag, which she shook in his face.

"Know what this is?" she said. He made a grab for it, but she snatched it away and threw it to Ellie. "It's evidence, that's what it is. It's proof that you tried to kill my cat!"

"Now hold on a minute. Calm down," he said, looking around as if he didn't want the neighbours to hear. "Nothing wrong with putting out a bit of cat food now and then, is there?"

"Why would you feed cats when you don't even like them?" Ellie demanded.

He moved towards her. "Give that to me, young lady. That's my property. I could have you done for theft and trespass and breaking and entering…"

Ellie was too quick for him. She darted down the garden, ready to run out into the alley. Jackie said, "We're going to take it to a vet we know. He'll soon find out if it's poisonous. And then the RSPCA will prosecute you, and your name will be in the paper."

"And none of the neighbours will ever speak to you again," I said.

Suddenly all the fight went out of him. "No," he said. "Don't do that, please – don't prosecute me."

"Why not?" said Ellie angrily. "You don't deserve to be let off – not after what you did to all those cats."

"I only did it for the sake of my garden," he said. "They drive me mad, cats do. Treat my garden like a toilet. Dig up my flower beds. And then give me a cheeky look, as if to say, we do what we like and you can't stop us. So I thought, right…"

Jackie said, "But there are ways of keeping them out. Machines to make sounds that annoy them… plants with scent they don't like…"

"Water pistols," I put in.

Ellie said, "There's no need to actually *kill* them. And poison is so cruel. A slow, painful death…"

"All right, all right," he said. "I shouldn't have done it. If I promise never to do it again…" He hesitated.

"Yes?" said Jackie.

"Would you let me off? Not take me to court? I swear I won't do it again."

Jackie was silent for a long moment.

"OK, here's what we'll do," she said at last. "We'll take the cat food to the vet and get it tested. We won't tell him where we found it… not yet."

She fixed him with a cat-like glare. "But if ever we hear of another cat being poisoned, then it will all come out. We'll tell the RSPCA, the neighbours, the newspapers – everyone."

"It won't happen," he said. "Believe me – it won't."

"Do you think he meant it?" I asked Ellie the next day.

She nodded. "I think he's dead scared of people finding out about him. Knowing what he's really like."

Yes – I knew the feeling.

"We got it all wrong," said Ellie. "The Bird Woman looked kind of weird and scary, but actually she was harmless. And Mr Whitely looked harmless, but all the time he was a poisoner."

"Like you said – don't judge by appearances."

She said, "That's the problem. People *do* judge by appearances all the time. They fancy someone good-looking without finding out what the person's actually like..."

"Boys do that," I said. "Girls don't. Or not as much."

"Oh sure," she said. "You only ever loved Leo for his mind."

"Shhh," I hissed. Leo was only a few feet away, at the back of the school minibus. Ellie and I were further forward, near an empty seat where Miranda should have been.

It was Friday evening; we were going to London to see a Christian theatre group perform. Mr Price had arranged the trip ages ago for any CU members who were interested. "Theatre group performing in London" had sounded quite glamorous. The disappointing reality was a church hall in Tooting, with rows of saggy seats around a square empty stage.

But when the show started it was actually rather good. There were several fast-moving comedy sketches that made me laugh out loud. One was about people at a party, with their thoughts – quite unlike their spoken words – being revealed by a voice-over.

"Fiona, how lovely! Long time no see!" (I can't stand her. I've been avoiding her for months.)

"I just love your dress, darling." (It's great – it makes her bum look twice the size of mine.)

"Dennis! And who's this beautiful young lady?" (Dirty old man. He's old enough to be her grandfather.)

No one said what they really thought. They all hid hateful, envious or critical feelings behind pleasant smiles. Everyone does it, I realised... everyone in the whole world. We all put on a good appearance to hide what we're really like.

The onstage party came to an end. The host said fond goodbyes, while thinking "Aren't they ever going to leave?" The lights went out. A moment's pause, then the all-knowing voice spoke again. The words were from the Bible:

"Man looks at the outward appearance. God looks at the heart."

Suddenly, sitting in the darkness, I felt as if a searchlight was focused on me. "God looks at the heart." In front of other people I might pretend to be nicer than I really was – but I couldn't fool God. He knew me inside out. He knew I was full of anger, jealousy, selfishness, greed...

Even my prayers had been selfish. "Oh God, please make me lose weight. Instantly, effortlessly, please. Then everyone will like me and I'll get a boyfriend – and I might even believe in you." No wonder those prayers hadn't been answered.

I dragged my attention back to the stage, where another act had begun. This one was not being played for laughs. A young girl ran away from home, looking for excitement in the bright lights of the city. But soon all her money was gone. She ended up sleeping rough, begging and stealing to get money for drugs. Her life was a total mess.

At last, in despair, she decided to go home. She would tell her parents how sorry she was – if they would listen. They would probably be furious with her. They might not even let her into the house.

But her parents had never stopped loving her and longing for her return. When they saw her at the gate they ran to meet her, hugging her so tightly that she was lifted off her feet. They welcomed her home; they cooked her favourite meal.

This began to sound familiar. Of course – it was like the story Jesus told about the Prodigal Son. And what was the meaning of that?

God loves us. He never stops loving us, even when we go far away from him. And as soon as we turn back to him, he opens his arms, he comes running to meet us…

"Oh God," I prayed silently, "is it true? Do you mean me? I'm sorry, I really am. I've messed up totally…"

I thought about my life, outwardly Christian – going to church, saying the right things, knowing the Bible – but inwardly just the opposite. Most of the time I hadn't been doing what God wanted, only what I wanted.

"Help me! I want to come back to you. I want to belong to you… really belong, on the inside as well as the outside."

I never expected what happened next – a surge of pure joy that swept over me. Like a huge ocean wave, strong yet gentle, happiness took hold of me and lifted me up. It was like being drowned in sheer delight. Amazing! Then the moment passed. The wave rolled on, leaving my feet on the ground again.

But I felt quite different from before. I felt as if I'd been washed clean. All the bad things I'd ever done, all the things I felt ashamed of – they were gone. Washed away… gone for ever.

Chapter Nineteen

Refugee

It was pouring with rain as we drove home, but I didn't care. I knew I had a big crazy grin on my face. Ellie gave me some funny looks, as if she was thinking, "OK, the show was good. But not *that* good."

Maybe later I would tell her what had happened – not yet, though. I didn't want to spoil it by talking about it.

Ellie nudged me. "We'll be there in ten minutes. You should ring your dad." The minibus was taking us back to school, where Dad would pick us up.

On the edge of town the bus slowed down at a roundabout, and I glanced out of the window. A lonely figure stood under a street light, trying to hitch a lift out of town. He'd be lucky. No one picks up hitch-hikers in the pouring rain.

I looked again, and gasped. It was a girl, not a boy. It was Miranda.

Miranda! What was she doing out here, all alone on a dark, wet night? Did her mother know? Stupid question.

The minibus swung round the roundabout, leaving the dark figure behind. "Did you see that?" I whispered to Ellie.

"See what?"

"That hitch-hiker by the roundabout. I'm almost sure it was Miranda."

"You what?" She gaped at me. "Like Miranda's going to be out here at almost midnight, in the pouring rain, when she's been grounded for weeks."

Yes, I knew it was unlikely, but – "Maybe she's

running away from home," I said. "Just like her brother did."

We stopped outside the school. I hurried Ellie out of the bus and into our car, where I told Dad what I thought I'd seen. "I'm not 100 per cent sure it was her. But can we go and see?"

"Yes, of course," Dad said.

Running away – where would she go? To London, probably, the place where most runaways end up, like mud settling on the bottom of a river. The big city… excitement… danger. Living on the streets when the money runs out, cold, hungry and desperate… Maybe, like her brother, she would never come back. No one would know if she was alive or dead.

We would have to try and stop her. But would she listen to us?

We were coming to the roundabout. Under the street lamp, the pavement was empty. Someone must have picked her up; we were too late.

Then, a hundred yards away, I saw a car at the roadside. Next to it something odd was going on – a fight, it looked like. Dad drove closer, and now I could see Miranda struggling with two men. They were trying to push her into the back of their car.

Dad slammed the brakes on. "Stay inside," he warned us, getting out. Then he yelled, "What do you think you're doing? Let go of her!"

Everything seemed to freeze for an instant. The two men stared at Dad, sizing him up. Their faces looked hard and mean. Dad was tall and pretty strong – but it was two against one.

Oh God! Please help us! Don't let them hurt him –

Your phone. The thought seemed to come out of nowhere, calm and clear.

Frantically I grabbed my mobile. I got out, holding it up so the men could see it. "If you don't let her go RIGHT NOW," I shouted, "I'm calling the police."

One of them swore. He shoved Miranda away so that she fell sprawling onto the ground. "Come on, leave it," he snarled. "I'm out of here."

His friend started to argue, then changed his mind as I began to dial 999. They both jumped into their car. With a slam of doors and a screech of tyres, they made off. Too late, I thought about getting their car number; their tail lights had vanished in the rain and the dark.

Miranda lay where she had fallen, sobbing bitterly. We helped her up; she was shivering with cold and shock. Her clothes were soaked, her hair was so wet that it stuck to her skull. Smudged make-up darkened her face like a bruise.

"It's all right," Dad said, "they've gone. And you'll soon be safely home." Miranda didn't have the strength to argue with him. She collapsed in the back of the car.

"What happened?" Ellie asked her. "Who were those men?"

"Two drunks," she muttered. "They stopped to give me a lift, but I didn't like the look of them, so I said no thanks."

"And then they tried to force you into the car?" I said.

She nodded. "If you hadn't come along..." Her voice shook.

"But where were you going?" Ellie demanded.

"I was leaving home. Running away." She sounded helpless and defeated, like a captured prisoner of war.

"Why?"

"Why do you think?" she flared up. "Because I can't stand it any more! Because my parents hate me!"

That was a bit extreme, I thought. Miranda's mum

didn't *hate* her. As for her dad, who could tell? He was a silent man, hard to get to know. Perhaps he hadn't always been so quiet before he met his wife.

"You don't know what it's like," Miranda said bitterly. "Ever since that party… I've said I'm sorry dozens of times, but she still goes on and on at me. How I've let her down. How much she's had to pay to get things fixed. How she hates my friends. How I'll end up just like my brother…"

Dad said, "But that doesn't mean she hates you. Just the opposite, I'd say. She's worried about you, she cares about you."

Miranda scowled. "Maybe. But only when I do as she tells me. She wants me to be good and obedient and go to church all the time and do well at school. But now she's found out I'm not like that… and she hates me."

I didn't know what to say. It could be there was some truth in what Miranda said. It could be that her mother longed to have a perfect daughter so that other people would see her as the perfect mother. (Judging by appearances again.) But Miranda had smashed that sweet-smiling, perfect image to bits.

I always used to envy Miranda's beauty and self-confidence. Looking at her now, there wasn't much to envy. And I had something she didn't have… I knew for certain that my parents loved me. Suddenly I felt quite sorry for her.

As we approached Miranda's house, she seemed to shrink down into her seat. "I'm going to be in so much trouble," she muttered.

The house was all in darkness. Her parents must be sound asleep, quite unaware that their Prodigal Daughter had returned (or even that she'd gone away).

Ellie suggested, "You could sneak back in, go to bed

and pretend it never happened."

"I haven't got a key," she said in that flat, hopeless voice. "I didn't think I was coming back."

Dad opened his door. "If your mum and dad are asleep," he said to Miranda, "they might not answer the door straight away. Why don't you wait in the car? It'll be warmer than shivering on the doorstep."

Clever old Dad, I thought to myself. He wants to explain the situation before Miranda's mum starts having a go at her.

He rang the doorbell. We waited silently; the only sound was the patter of rain on the roof. Dad rang again, and a light went on upstairs. After a minute the door opened an inch or two, allowing him to talk to someone inside. At last the door was opened wide. We could see the hall, brightly lit, with two dressing-gowned figures in the doorway. They both stood there watching as Dad came back to the car and helped Miranda out.

She looked awful – wet, shivering, as pale as death. She walked with her head down, like a refugee in some war-torn country, afraid to go on, afraid to go back. Her father moved aside silently to let her in.

Wait a minute! It's not supposed to be like that! What about the joyous welcome, running to meet her, hugging her? I could see from her mother's face what sort of welcome was in store. Mrs Frost looked ready to explode with fury. (But not in public. She would wait until the door was shut.)

Dad came back to the car, looking rather grim. "Didn't you *tell* them?" I said.

"You know what Mary's like," he said. "I didn't get the chance to say anything much."

"But she'll tear Miranda apart! Miranda doesn't need telling off, she needs..." I struggled to put it into words.

What Miranda needed, apart from a warm bath, a hot drink and some sleep, was... to feel loved. To know that her parents still loved her – she was still their daughter, no matter what.

"She'll run away again," I said, sure of it. "Next time she'll plan it better, and she'll succeed. Just like her brother." If only there was something we could do...

The thought came: There is something you could do. You could own up about the party.

No! I can't do that! And anyway, how would it help?

You never know. If you take your share of the blame, Miranda's parents might not be so angry with her.

OK, OK. I will. But not tonight... I'll do it some other day.

No. Do it now.

Look, I did say I would do what you wanted, not what I wanted. And I meant it. But I didn't realise it would be so hard...

Slowly, reluctantly, I got out of the car.

Chapter Twenty

Not again

It was tougher than a twenty-mile run, scarier than a leap off the top diving board. It was the hardest thing I'd ever done – simply walking up that path and ringing the bell.

"Phoebe! What are you doing?" Dad called, and I heard the car door open. Oh no… I would have to say it all in front of Dad. That made things even worse.

Miranda's father, opening the door, looked surprised to see me.

"There's something I have to tell you," I said.

"Yes?" His face looked guarded. Maybe he expected to hear more about Miranda's misdeeds.

"It's just that…" The words seemed to stick in my throat. I stared hard at the front door, which had coloured glass panes in it. (One of them didn't quite match the others – perhaps as a result of the party.)

I started again. "You know the fight at the party? It wasn't Miranda's fault… it was mine. I told that boy Smurf that Miranda had invited him, but I made that up. I knew he would cause trouble – I wanted him to. And I'm really sorry."

He stared at me.

"I'll help to pay for the damage," I babbled on. "I just want you to know that Miranda had nothing to do with it."

Mr Frost didn't react at all – which was scary. He turned and called to his wife, "Mary! Could you come here for a minute?"

Miranda's mum came down the stairs. When she saw

me, an automatic smile flickered onto her face like a pale fluorescent light. "Phoebe! How nice to…"

How nice to see you, she'd been about to say. It was automatic, like the smile. But Mr Frost interrupted, "Phoebe has something to tell us."

I said my piece all over again, watching her face change from surprise to anger, then to a grim, closed look that gave nothing away.

"So you see, it wasn't Miranda's fault," I said.

"I disagree," she snapped. "Miranda shouldn't have arranged the party in the first place. She shouldn't have told all those lies. She shouldn't have been drinking. She knew how wrong it was."

"But she said she's sorry," I pleaded. "Can't you forgive her?"

"Not until she's changed her ways. And she obviously hasn't done that. The fact that she tried to run away…"

"Oh, can't you just *listen* for a minute?" I cried. "She told us why she ran away. It's because she thinks you don't love her."

This, I could see, was a bigger shock than anything else I'd said. Miranda's mother looked as if I'd hit her smack in the eye. For a second or two – amazingly – she was lost for words.

"But we *do* love her, of course we do," she said. "She's our whole life. That's why we want her to –"

I went on recklessly, "Miranda feels as if you only love her when she's good. If she does something bad, you hate her."

Mr Frost gave his wife a long, silent look, as if to say: I've been trying to tell you this for ages, but you wouldn't listen.

I said, "In Sunday school, when we were little, you taught us about how God loves us. You said he never stops loving us and he forgives us if we're sorry for what we did. Well, Miranda's really sorry. So am I. Can't you forgive us?"

I thought I had almost got through to her. Then her face grew hostile again.

"Thank you, Phoebe," she said stiffly. "But I hardly think I need lessons from a child on how to bring up my own daughter. And now, if you'll excuse us – it's getting late." In one smooth motion, she shut the door.

Dad, who had been standing right behind me, put his arm round me. "Well done," he whispered. "You said all the things I ought to have said earlier."

"But it won't make any difference," I said, feeling choked.

"I wouldn't be too sure… What was all that about the party?"

Once again I explained. Dad looked grave. "We'll talk about it in the morning. And you're right – we should pay for some of the damage."

He said *we*, not *you*. He was on my side.

To my surprise, Miranda turned up at youth group on Sunday. Even greater surprise – she came towards me, smiling.

"I don't know what you told my mum," she said. "But she's been all right about the other night. I thought she would kill me."

"That's great! I don't mean great that she would kill you…"

Miranda laughed. "And I had a good talk with Dad. He said that if I really don't want to change schools, I don't have to. Because that was another reason I ran away… I was scared of going to St Margaret's."

That surprised me too. Maybe Miranda wasn't as

confident as I'd always thought she was. Her self-assurance was like a snail shell – it looked tough but was actually quite fragile.

"So you're staying on at Sandersfield High?" I said, trying to sound pleased.

Miranda was not fooled. "Look, I'm sorry about… you know… all those things I said."

"Yes, well… I'm sorry about the party."

I didn't think I could ever be good friends with Miranda – we were so completely different. But in some ways I knew her better than anyone else in the room. Actually, in some ways we were quite alike… But the great thing was, we weren't enemies. Not any more.

I decided to stop dieting, or rather stop pretending to diet. It hadn't done me any good – I had lost weight but put it all back on again. Instead I would try to break the habit of eating whenever I felt bored, depressed, etc. Rather than reach for the biscuit tin, I would do something active such as taking a walk.

Food used to be my main comfort in life. Anxiety, loneliness, that 'no one loves me' feeling – they could all be banished by an orange Club biscuit. But only for about five minutes. Then they would come creeping back.

'No one loves me' is a lie; I have to keep remembering that. Mum and Dad love me, although being human, they don't always show it. And God loves me. Not like Miranda's mum – 'I'll love you if you're good.' Not like most boys – 'I'll love you if you look good.' He loves me – good or bad, fat or thin.

Ellie rang me. "Do you want the good news or the bad news?"

"Give me the bad news first."

"Leo's got a girlfriend."

"Oh. What's the good news?" I asked.

"She likes skateboarding. So with any luck she'll break a leg and be in hospital for months."

"She can have him," I said carelessly. "I've gone off him." It was true, because this really nice guy had started coming to youth group. He was tall and fair, with a wicked smile and a crazy sense of humour. Jack, his name was.

Miranda, with her radar tracking system for Grade A boys, had noticed him at once. And he had noticed her. Well, he could hardly miss her – she had arranged herself like a film star posing for the cameras, showing off her face, her slim figure, her perfect legs...

Suddenly I felt a desperate longing for some chocolate. I pushed the thought firmly away. "Don't suppose you fancy taking a walk?" I said to Ellie.

"Not *again*."

But she's a good friend – she came with me. We walked round the block in the evening sunlight, noticing several cats out and about, enjoying their freedom. Mr Whitely was hoeing his garden as we passed. We ignored each other.

There was a FOR SALE sign outside the Bird Woman's house. She had moved to a nursing home, because her stroke had left her unable to walk properly. Ellie and I had been to visit her there. She had a room with a view of the gardens, where she could still look at birds. Next time I went to see her, I would take her some bird seed.

As we passed the dark, empty house, Ellie quickened her step. I kept pace with her quite easily. Maybe I was getting a tiny bit fitter with all this walking.

Ellie said, "Did I tell you about the Three Monkeys?

Their babysitter swears she's never going back."

"Why? Whatever happened?"

"When Adam was supposed to be in bed, he sneaked out with his skateboard. He totally vanished for ages. The babysitter was going frantic – she rang Suzanne. Dad and Suzanne rushed home, and just then Adam strolled in going 'What's all the fuss about?'"

I started to laugh. "It isn't funny," Ellie wailed. "Dad wants *me* to babysit next time."

"He must have a short memory. Why don't you just say no?"

"Because he said he'd pay me double the normal rate," she muttered. "He said he'd give you the same if you come too."

"What? He's prepared to pay *four times* the normal rate?"

"He's pretty desperate. It's their wedding anniversary soon, and no other babysitter in town will go near the place."

I thought for a while. But then what are friends for? And the money would be nice. I was flat broke after paying for that broken glass.

"OK," I said. "After all, it can't possibly be worse than the last time. Can it?"

If you've enjoyed this book, look out for three more great books about Phoebe!

Reasons why I can't have more pocket money according to Mum and Dad:

1 Because money can't buy happiness (true, but it does mean you can be miserable in comfort).

2 Because Dad is a teacher, not a multi-millionaire.

3 Because when he was my age he only got 15p a year, blah blah blah.

4 Because if I got extra money, my sister would have to get some too, or it wouldn't be fair.

5 Because if I'm so desperate, why don't I get a paper round or something?

6 Because it's time I learned that money doesn't grow on trees (if only!).

Money makes people do crazy things, but how far will Phoebe and Ellie go to get some extra cash?
ISBN 1 85999 700 7

Mum asks me, "If everyone else jumped over a cliff, would you do it too?"

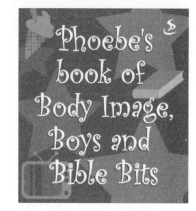

A Yes, if it looked like they were having a good time on the way down

B Yes, because I'd be so lonely without any friends left

C No, because my mum would make me wait until I'm older

Get great advice from fabulous Phoebe (and the Bible!) in this essential survival book!

ISBN 1 85999 663 9

Phoebe's book of Body Image, Boys and Bible Bits

How to relieve peer pressure – some suggestions:

Kathy Lee

A Don't have any friends
B Become known for being slightly weird, but harmless
C Fight back. Stand firm. Defend your principles, quoting 23 different Bible verses (then see A above)
D Just give in, go with the flow, and become identical to everyone else.

After all, does it really matter?

Phoebe faces her biggest challenge yet as she tries to stand out in the crowd (for reasons other than her size). But when you're dealing with French exchange students, embarrassing school dances and mysterious thefts it's hard to keep your mind on doing the right thing!
ISBN 1 85999 701 5

You can buy these books at your local Christian bookshop, or online at www.scriptureunion.org.uk/publishing or call Mail Order direct 08450 706 006